When they got to th  a big smile.

But Nolan looked intense as he pushed the button to call the elevator.

"Is everything okay?"

"No."

That surprised her. She'd thought her presentation had gone really well. "Why not?"

He took her hand and drew her away from the elevator and away from the offices. "I wasn't planning on hiring you."

"What? Why not?"

He cursed under his breath and then shook his head. "I want you, Delaney. And I never mix business and pleasure."

"I do," she said, going up on her tiptoes and doing what she'd wanted to do since she'd seen him in his office.

* * *

The Billionaire Plan by Katherine Garbera
is part of The Image Project series.

Dear Reader,

I hope you are enjoying The Image Project series. I'm so excited for Delaney's story. If I'm being totally honest, she's my favorite of the three heroines. She was just so much fun to write. She's mischievous and flawed, but has a really good heart, so I knew her hero had to be someone really special too.

Nolan is a single dad who works hard and plays hard. He's working in a cutting-edge field designing projects for space missions to Mars. When these two meet, sparks fly...but Delaney's got some information that she probably shouldn't have and Nolan has to consider his daughter. He's never been a man to parade women through Daisey's life but neither Nolan nor Delaney can keep their hands off each other.

I hope you enjoy reading this story as much as I enjoyed writing it!

Happy reading,

Katherine

KATHERINE GARBERA

THE BILLIONAIRE PLAN

HARLEQUIN
DESIRE

HARLEQUIN®
DESIRE™

Recycling programs
for this product may
not exist in your area.

ISBN-13: 978-1-335-58160-0

The Billionaire Plan

Harlequin Enterprises ULC
22 Adelaide St. West, 41st Floor
Toronto, Ontario M5H 4E3, Canada
www.Harlequin.com

Printed in U.S.A.

Katherine Garbera is the *USA TODAY* bestselling author of more than a hundred and twenty-five books. She's a sucker for a happy ending, believes in the power of falling in love and the deep bonds of friendship. Her books are known for their emotional complexity and sizzling sensuality. She lives in the midlands of the UK with her own Mr. Right. You can find her on the web at www.katherinegarbera.com and on Instagram and Facebook.

Books by Katherine Garbera

Harlequin Desire

One Night

One Night with His Ex
One Night, Two Secrets
One Night to Risk It All
Her One Night Proposal

Destination Wedding

The Wedding Dare
The One from the Wedding
Secrets of a Wedding Crasher

The Image Project

Billionaire Makeover
The Billionaire Plan

Visit her Author Profile page at Harlequin.com, or katherinegarbera.com, for more titles.

You can also find Katherine Garbera on Facebook, along with other Harlequin Desire authors, at Facebook.com/harlequindesireauthors!

This one is for my sweet little Godiva,
who we sadly lost at the end of January.
She was my faithful writing companion
and just my heart. I still miss her.

Special thanks to Stacy Boyd for shepherding
this series through all of the stages.
It's always fun to work with you
and I love your insights.

One

Delaney Alexander ignored the stares and whispered comments as she entered the church and looked around for a friendly face. A lot of the people she knew, even her extended family, wouldn't have given her a second glance; she knew she was a social pariah right now. She'd read the latest in Wend-Z City about herself.

Ugh.

That was all she had to say about that. She had almost heeded her father's advice and skipped the wedding, but hiding at home went against the grain. She was tired of lying low. Her entire life she'd been moving, going, doing things. She knew that at times her lifestyle came across as crazy, but she didn't mind. She'd always lived by her own rules.

Until Malcolm Quell had come into her life. He'd

told he loved her—*lie*. The slimy executive had said that they would make each other stronger—*another lie*. And he'd told her he wanted to find investors for his business—*truth*. But worst of all? He'd declared to the world that she wasn't enough for him—*maybe true*?

She'd started out angry at Malcolm. Angry that he'd broken up with her publicly by dumping all her stuff on his front doorstep. Angry that he'd moved on so quickly with a socialite that was five years younger and arguably hotter. Angry that her beloved dog Stanley still liked the rat.

But that had changed when she'd learned that he had some shady business deals thanks to an offhand comment and a raid of his personal safe. Sure, she'd been arrested for trespassing and everyone from Wend-Z City's gossip website to strangers on the street thought she was a woman with a grudge who couldn't get over her ex. But it was all worth it because Delaney had the goods on Malcolm.

And she was one step away from finding the leverage to stop his illegal business dealings and getting the closure she needed. She'd always heard that the perfect revenge was a life lived well, which sounded like bullshit too. The perfect revenge was getting back at the person who hurt her and rubbing their nose in it.

Which was entirely what she intended to do with Malcolm. But she had to get through today. Put on a smile and show the world that she'd indeed moved on.

She felt a little hand on hers and glanced down into a pair of big brown eyes ringed with the thickest, blackest eyelashes she'd ever seen. Delaney crouched to be at the girl's eye level.

"Hi there," she murmured. "Are you okay?"

The little girl crinkled her forehead. "Pamela? My daddy said he'd be right in and I'm supposed to stay with you," she said.

"Sorry, I'm not Pamela. I'm Delaney, who are you?" she asked with a gentle smile. As a child, Delaney had attended a lot of adult functions with her father, and she'd been lost more than once.

"Daisey. Daddy said look for the prettiest blonde lady, and I spotted you."

Delaney was beginning to really like this kid and not just because she called her pretty. "Don't worry. I'll help you find Pamela. There are a lot of pretty ladies here today. Including you."

The child gave a little twirl, letting the full skirt of her dress fan out around her legs. "My dress is very swirly. They are my favorite kind."

Delaney stood up as she said, "Mine too. So, Pamela has blond hair?"

Daisey nodded several times.

More people were entering the vestibule of the church and now that she wasn't alone, Delaney didn't mind entering the church. She pushed aside the censure she knew she'd get from those in attendance.

"Do you know the bride or the groom?" she asked the little girl as they moved forward in search of Pamela.

"The groom. He works for my daddy," Daisey explained.

Delaney hadn't met the groom. The bride was her

cousin, but she wasn't particularly close to her. In fact, she was really just here to try to meet one of the guests. Nolan Cooper. He was a competing businessman who had been slowly moving in on Quell Aerospace's government contracts. And the key to her getting closure and making things right. Delaney was hoping to bump into him, share some of the information she'd taken from Malcolm's safe to give Cooper Aeronautical a leg up. Because there was no way that Cooper was going to beat Malcolm legitimately from what Delaney had seen.

When they got to the beginning of the church aisle, the groomsmen asked if they were guests of the bride or groom. The church was festooned with more pink flowers than Delaney had ever seen. Her cousin had gone a bit overboard.

"One of each. I'm helping this little lady find her family. And she's with the groom," Delaney said.

"The groom's family is being seated on the right if you want to go and have a look," he offered.

"Thanks," Delaney said, looking up at the large church, which was already half full.

"Can I escort you two?" he asked.

She looked down at Daisey who just shook her head. Seeming afraid of the other man and the crowded church, the little girl's hand tightened in Delaney's.

"We've got this," she told the usher and then started up the aisle. Daisey stopped her with a tug on her hand. She looked down at her.

"You know the bride?" Daisey asked.

Delaney nodded, skimming the rows for a blonde lady and finding several, but she wasn't exactly sure if any of them were Pamela. She noticed her father had spotted her, and she saw his brow furrow as he met her gaze. She turned away, stooping to Daisey's level again. "I've spotted three blonde ladies, but I'm not sure which one is Pamela. Maybe we should go to the front and just wait for your daddy."

She nodded, then leaned in close, putting her hand on Delaney's arm to whisper, "Everyone is staring."

Delaney glanced around and realized that it wasn't just her father who had noticed them. "That's because you're so beautiful and everyone is trying to figure out who you are."

Daisey giggled. "Daddy says the same thing."

"He must be really smart," Delaney said. "Best to pretend we don't notice those other people and just go wait for you father," she said, standing again and turning with Daisey's hand clasped in hers. As she did so, she bumped into a very tall man who was wearing some delicious-smelling cologne, a scowl on his handsome face and eyes with the same thick lashes as Daisey's.

"Daisey's daddy?" she asked, tipping her head to the side.

"Indeed, and you are?"

"A pretty blonde lady according to Daisey," Delaney said wryly.

"Daddy!" Daisey exclaimed, wrapping her arms around her father's legs. "Delaney was trying to help me find Pamela, but there are a lot of blonde ladies."

"That's my fault, Pip," he said, scooping her up into his big, strong arms. "Thank you for your help, Delaney."

"It was my pleasure," she said.

He stood so close that even though she knew the eyes of everyone in the church were on them, she couldn't bring herself to look away. His eyes were intense, a dark brown color that mesmerized her. She wasn't sure what to say to him. She wanted to just keep staring at his face, which wasn't classically handsome but so compelling.

"I owe you one," he said, his voice a deep rumble that sent shivers down her spine.

"It was nothing. I enjoyed having Daisey by my side." She tipped her head to smile at his daughter.

"Nolan! Over here," a woman called.

Nolan? Nolan Cooper? It had to be. How many Nolans would be at the wedding? She realized she was still staring at him, and he raised one eyebrow at her as if to say he'd noticed.

Delaney glanced over and realized the woman was Pamela Donahue, owner of the Donahue gallery and a graphic artist. Delaney had a print of her *Troubled Waters* lithograph hanging on the wall of her living room. "Seems you've found your lady. Goodbye, Daisey. And Nolan? Nice to have met you."

"Nolan Cooper," he said, holding his hand out to her.

She took it and felt a little tingle go up her arm. "Delaney Alexander."

"I know," he said with a wink. "Thanks again."

He moved toward his seat, and she realized she was still watching him go. *Get a grip, Delaney.* Turning, she walked toward the back of the church. She wasn't about to go and sit with her father, so she stepped into the first empty pew, took a seat and settled herself in for the wedding. Despite everything, she was very glad that she'd decided to come today—and not just because it irritated her father. She'd needed a casual way to meet Nolan Cooper and now she had. For the first time since she'd been arrested for trespassing, she realized that she might be on the right track.

Nolan wasn't what she'd been expecting. He was huge for one thing, tall and muscly, and even though he'd been wearing a tailored suit, she'd noticed. The man had a square jaw and thick, dark hair and eyebrows…and there was something about him that left her unsettled. He exuded animal magnetism in spades, but it was *more* than that.

He'd looked at her, and she almost felt like he'd really seen her. Not many people did. Which could prove to be a problem. Because if he could read her so well, just from one meeting, she wasn't sure how she was going to be able to manipulate him into doing what she needed done. She wasn't going to alter her plan, but the truth was, she might need to do a bit more research on him.

Of course, Delaney had never met a man she couldn't bring around to her way of thinking. Not her autocratic father, not most of her boyfriends, and she certainly wasn't going to let Nolan Cooper be the first man to steer her off course.

Pamela Donahue hadn't stayed for the wedding reception, and if Nolan was being brutally honest, he was glad. They'd been set up by a mutual friend, and there was no denying that she was beautiful, smart and funny. But the fact that she hadn't waited at the entrance for

Daisey, as she'd said she would, had made her less attractive to him. His daughter was six and the center of his world. He worked hard, played hard, but his most important role was being Daisey's dad. His wife, Merri, had died during a complicated childbirth. So it had always just been the two of them.

He usually didn't introduce women into their lives but since it was a wedding, he'd broken his own rule. Something he wouldn't do again. He wasn't a second chances kind of guy.

The reception was in a large banquet hall. The decor was all pink and white, and Daisey had told him twice that when she got married, she wanted to wear a flower wreath like the bride had. He agreed she could have her dream wedding.

Daisey kept circling all of the tables at the reception instead of picking one for them to sit at. The bride and groom had decided on an open seating plan for anyone not in the family or bridal party. It took him a moment to realize that his daughter was looking for someone. He was pretty sure that someone was Delaney Alexander, mainly because Daisey hadn't stopped talking about her since they'd gotten into the car to drive to the reception.

"Pip, we are going to have to pick a table," he said.

"I know, Daddy. I was just hoping…"

"Hoping for what?" asked Delaney.

They both turned as Delaney came up next to them. Daisey squealed and hugged the woman's legs. Delaney hugged her right back. She was wearing a robin's-egg blue dress with a full tulle skirt and fitted bodice. Her blond hair was worn down to frame her heart-shaped face, and she had on a tiny-diamond-encrusted head-band and matching pendant. "If you two don't mind, could I sit with you?"

"Yes!"

"Sure," he agreed with his daughter. "Will this table do?"

He gestured to the one behind them. Delaney nodded enthusiastically. "It's perfect."

His six-year-old went and stood by a chair, and Nolan pulled it out for her and helped seat her. She started to play with the small party favors on the table as he turned back to Delaney. He knew about her. Who *hadn't* heard of her, right?

The poor little rich girl. Dish Soap Heiress and scandalous socialite. So basically, he knew nothing about the actual woman, just lots of gossip and hearsay.

Except that she'd been nice to his daughter twice. And a lot of other women wouldn't have been. He wasn't sure if it was genuine, but he'd keep his eye on her. One thing, given her fortune, he ruled out was that she wanted something from him.

"Where's Pamela?"

"She had another engagement," he said.

"Oh, that's too bad. I was hoping to talk to her. I love her art," Delaney murmured. "But I'm glad I ran into the two of you. I wasn't looking forward to making small talk today."

He wasn't sure what she meant by that. "Do you not intend to talk to me?"

"*What?* Oh, yes. Sorry! I just meant with strangers. You and I are old friends now," she said with a wink.

She was cute. He had already known that from her photos but her personality…he was surprised that someone who was allegedly obsessed with her ex would be so bubbly and fun.

"Are we now?"

"For my part, yes. But then there aren't many friendly faces in this room."

He lifted a bemused brow. "The bride is your cousin. Half your family is here. I spoke to your father a few minutes ago."

"My point exactly."

He laughed but then realized that beneath her bubbly smile there was a bit of nervous energy. "Why are you here, then?"

"I'll never let the bast—" She broke off as she looked down at Daisey. "Well, you know, I won't let them get me down."

He had the same attitude toward life. "Me either. But usually for me the situation is more business related than weddings."

"Two different worlds," she said. "What's your business?"

"Daddy is going to send us to Mars," Daisey declared. "Aren't you?"

"That's the plan," he said. "Can I get you a drink from the bar?"

"Champagne," Delaney replied.

"Shirley Temple?" he asked his daughter.

"Yes, please. Delaney and I will save your seat."

"Thanks," he said, ruffling her hair before turning to go and get their drinks.

He knew a lot of the people in the room. The groom, Jay Park, was one of his lead engineers at Cooper Aeronautical. The rest of the engineering team was seated at various tables. He'd make sure to talk to all his employees before the night was over. There was a lot of Chicago's upper society here as well as the bride, Hana Mallory, who was related to the Alexanders.

He waited in line at the bar to get their refreshments, wondering why Delaney didn't feel welcomed by her family. Maybe the arrest? He'd heard she'd been apprehended for trespassing back in July. But since Malcolm Quell had agreed not to press charges, that had sort of gone away.

When he got back to the table, Daisey was still talking a mile a minute to Delaney, who had her head bent toward his daughter's, listening intently. He stopped for a second, not sure he liked the closeness that was developing between Daisey and this stranger. She had an ethereal beauty that he couldn't stop thinking about. The dress she wore in essence reminded him of Daisey's, but Delaney was all woman. The fitted bodice hugged her full breasts and nipped in her waist before falling over her hips and ending midcalf. As gorgeous as she was, they didn't know her, and for all he knew they'd never see her again. He had no idea how Daisey would react to that. She'd been surprisingly clingy lately and he'd put it down to her starting at a new school and first grade, but was it something else?

His own mom had died three years before Daisey was born and he had a nanny and housekeeper who helped out around the house, but basically, he and Daisey were on their own. Nolan liked it that way. He didn't want to take a chance on her starting to rely on anyone else and having them taken away.

"Why such a serious face, dude? This is supposed to be a party."

Nolan smiled at one of the men who worked for him and nodded. "Just trying to remember if the bartender mixed the drinks right. Nice ceremony, wasn't it?"

His employee talked for a few more minutes and then waved him off as his date called him away. Nolan realized that he had to be more careful. He'd been spending a lot of time at work, innovating and finding new technologies that would make living on Mars not only possible but enjoyable. Not a survival experience but more of a welcome home one.

He shook his head. He was going to put himself between Daisey and Delaney and nip this friendship in the bud. His daughter didn't need to be friends with a scandalous socialite. Well, that sounded wrong, even to his own ears, but he had to protect her at all costs.

"Scoot over, Pip, I'll sit by Delaney," he said.

She frowned up at him and he raised both eyebrows. The silent exchange lasted longer than he'd expected it to as his stubborn daughter just kept frowning and he simply shook his head. She sighed. Then shifted over to the chair he'd pulled out for her.

"Thanks," he said, leaning down to kiss the top of Daisey's head and place her drink in front of her on the table. He handed the champagne glass to Delaney before he sat down between the two of them.

"Hey, Nolan, can we sit here?"

It was his assistant, Perri, and her husband, and six-year-old son, Thom. "Yes."

Thom sat next to Daisey, and his daughter was soon engaged in a conversation with the little boy. Nolan introduced Delaney to Perri.

"You're on my list of people to call on Monday," Perri said.

"She is? Why?" Nolan asked.

"She's part of IDG, the brand management company that the board voted to hire for our next rollout," Perri said.

"You are?" he asked, turning back to Delaney. Somehow the thought of her having a job was unexpected.

"I am. Surely you didn't think I was just the dish soap heiress?" she teased.

"No, I'd heard other things too," he said.

"Like what? Light stalking?"

He was surprised at her ability to joke about it, but in the same vein he admired that about her. "Yeah. I pretty much just know about the gossipy stuff and only that because Perri keeps the audio on her computer up so I hear it when she's in. So…what is it you could do for my company?" he asked, deciding a change of subject was in order.

"Well, I will be happy to send you over some information on Monday. But top level, I make you look like the best thing in space travel since Armstrong and Aldrin landed on the moon," she said.

"You can do that?" he asked, not sure that she could deliver on that promise, but willing to give her a chance.

She waggled her eyebrows at him and winked. "That's what I do."

Before he could ask any more questions, the emcee for the reception asked them all to stand and welcome the new Mr. and Mrs. Park. The reception turned out to be more fun than he'd expected, and the more he talked to Delaney the more he realized that he was intrigued by the woman behind the scandals.

Two

Light stalking.

It kept running through his head as they ate dinner and the conversation flowed around him. He noticed despite her apparent aversion for small talk, she was actually very good at it. His assistant, Perri, and her husband were charmed by Delaney as was everyone who came close to their table.

Except her father.

He noticed that H. Baxter Alexander glanced over with a scowl each time Delaney's laughter rang out. At first Nolan wasn't sure that she was aware of it, but then he realized she was deliberately being loud and seeming to enjoy getting a rise out of her old man because when her father turned away, she looked over at him.

"What's the deal with you and your dad?" he asked after one such incident.

"Huh?"

"Don't play dumb, it's insulting to both of us."

She smiled at him, and he felt something he wasn't going to acknowledge. She was too quick and clever by half. His gut was torn by the fact that he couldn't help but be enchanted by her even though he didn't really trust her.

"He told me to lie low until the press wasn't interested in me anymore and not to come to the wedding," she said. "I just never respond well to that kind of behavior."

He narrowed his eyes at her. She didn't sound repentant or defiant. "What behavior?"

"Ultimatums. I'm fairly sure that everyone reacts the same way."

"Not everyone," he said.

She arched a delicate brow. "Like you'd do what someone else said?"

"I wouldn't," he admitted gruffly. "But—"

"Don't you *dare* say you're a man," she warned him.

"I wasn't going to," he said, but he had been thinking that. He was also just a big guy at six foot five, and no one had told him what to do since his father had died. "I meant that if my dad were still here, I might reconsider."

"Were you close?" she asked curiously.

The Dish Soap Heiress was good at deflecting, he realized. She took a statement or question and sort of answered it and then asked one of her own. Clever, he reminded himself. So much more than a sexy body and gamine face.

"We were," he divulged. He still missed his father. It had taken him quite a few years to admit that. He'd been angry at his father for doing a risky job and not coming home from his last assignment. But once he'd been old enough to understand it, he'd…well, some would say mellowed.

"I'm sorry. When did he pass away?" she asked softly.

"When I was twelve," he said. Suddenly realizing he was doing all the talking. "But I read your mother died when you were a baby. So you grew up with just your father?"

She licked her lips and reached for her champagne flute and finished the glass. "I did, well, sort of. Mostly I grew up with nannies and then of course at boarding school. I hope you don't do that with Daisey."

"I won't." Not that it was any of her business.

"Good. Little girls need someone to listen to their dreams and stories. To be fair, little boys do too," she said with a wistful note to her voice.

He realized this was probably the most real that Delaney had been with him since they'd met. She was like a light reflection sparkling off a mirror, and every once in a while he saw through the glamour she wore like an armor to the real woman lurking beneath.

"Daddy, Thom and I want to have cake," Daisey said, leaning around his shoulder and smiling over at Delaney.

"I'll go and get you some," he replied. "Delaney?"

"Yes, please," she said. "And some more champagne."

"Certainly. Pip, another Shirley Temple?"

"Yes, please. Can Thom have a cherry Coke?"

"It's up to his mom and dad," Nolan said. He'd learned at the first play group that he'd taken Daisey to that he couldn't make decisions for other kids.

Thom turned to ask his parents and Delaney got up. "I'll go with you. You have big hands but even you might struggle to carry all of that."

"Thanks."

"Mom said I can have a Coke," Thom said.

"Great!" He turned to the boy's mother. "Perri, will you watch Daisey until I return?"

"Of course," she said with a smile.

"I've got two questions for you," Delaney said as they stood in line for the cake.

"Only *two*?"

"Well, for now," she said with a smile.

"Shoot."

"Why do you call Daisey Pip?"

He'd told himself he was going to keep it light and this question, though personal, wasn't really too revealing. "She was just this tiny little pip when she was born. When I held her in my arms, I used to call her my little pip-squeak. It sort of stuck."

"I love that! She's a very sweet little girl."

"She is right now, but when she's tired, she has a stubborn side," he admitted. He glanced back at the table where he saw his daughter talking very seriously to Thom. She was his world, and he wasn't going to pretend that she wasn't.

"Second question?"

"Why did you drop Daisey off by herself at the church? I know she was safe enough, but from what I've seen of you, that's not really your style."

He was surprised by her question. He gave her a long stare. "Because of your cousin's position in society I knew that the paparazzi would be here, and I don't want her picture in papers."

She gave him another of those disarming smiles of hers that made it hard for him to remember he didn't really trust her.

"I get that," she said quietly. "No one ever did that with me. I mean, how could they? My picture was used to launch the all-natural baby soap line and then Mom died…but I commend you for keeping her away from the press. I'll go get the drinks while you wait for the cake. Jack and Coke?"

"Yes," he answered. Before he could say anything else, she'd disappeared into the crowd. But he couldn't stop thinking of what Delaney had said. She'd been in the papers since the day she was born. Her life had been in front of the camera and on the gossip sites, all the ups and downs, highs and lows.

So that brought him back to what she'd said about light stalking. Delaney was too savvy to be caught un-awares. What had she really been up to at Malcolm Quell's, and was she after something from him? After all, they were both the only game in town when it came to aerospace.

For her entire life, Delaney had followed her own path. Looking out for herself because she'd realized early on that she'd had to. Oh, poor little Delaney, she thought dryly, not allowing herself to get caught in feeling sorry for herself. One of the pluses to that was that when she set her mind on something, she always made it happen. And she wasn't going to let this man with the broad shoulders, edgy smile that hinted of secrets, and those sinfully sexy brown eyes sway her.

She'd engineered this entire meeting to use the knowledge she'd found in her ex's safe to her advantage. A part of her wanted to see Malcolm fail, but more so she wanted the world to be fair.

Her father had told her more than once that it wasn't, but she'd always believed it should be. And she had a way to even the odds and give Nolan a level playing field...but there was something else going on here too. An emotion she couldn't or rather didn't *want* to identify. So, she ignored it. She'd accomplished her goal for today having met Nolan, and was now going to take the rest of the night for herself.

It didn't matter that he was doing everything in his power to protect his daughter. Something that H. Baxter Alexander had never considered. She told herself she was way over her daddy issues and had moved on. But she knew that was a lie.

She was okay with the white lies she told herself. Sometimes they helped her sleep at night, other times they made her erratic behavior sort of justifiable. But Nolan and Daisey...sure she needed him to get even with Malcolm. That didn't meant she couldn't be friends with them.

Right?

"Daughter."

She glanced over her shoulder to see her dad standing there. He had always seemed tall to her, but after standing next to Nolan for the last few minutes, her dad didn't seem quite as big.

"Father."

He shook his head and raised his eyebrows at her. He did that when he was ticked at her, but had to keep up appearances.

"The wedding was nice, wasn't it?" she asked. She wasn't going to apologize for showing up.

"It was a bit over the top, but your cousin has always been like that."

She smiled at the wry tone of his voice. Hana always had been one for the ostentatious look that shouted to the world she was wealthy.

"I did think there was a bit too much pink."

"Jones said it looked like Pepto," her father said.

"She's right. Did you really bring Jones as your date?" Delaney asked. "Jones" was Shireen Jones, her father's assistant and right hand. She had been with her father for the last fifteen years, and there were times when Delaney wondered if there was something more between them than boss-assistant, but neither had given anything away.

"I did. She's good company and she can handle any fires that come up, like if someone in the family who's getting lots of negative press shows up unexpectedly."

"Who would dare defy you?" she said glibly, moving forward in the line. She wasn't doing this. She wasn't going to apologize to her father. She was thirty years old, for Pete's sake!

"Apparently only you."

"Did you tell someone else not to show up?" she asked. "Really, Dad, you can't boss everyone around."

"Beg to differ, but the only one who doesn't listen to me is you."

She gave him a cheeky grin. "That's because I'm not intimidated by you."

He just shook his head and then glanced over to the table she'd been sitting at. "I hope you know what you are doing with Cooper. He's nothing like Malcolm."

She didn't need to hear this from him. "I know that, Dad. Thank God for that. He's got a cute little motherless daughter."

"I know. Does she remind you of yourself?" he asked. "Is that why you are hanging out with them? Tell me this has nothing to do with your arrest at Quell's mansion."

The person in front of her walked off with their drink order and she turned her back on her father, placing her own at the bar. Her father was baiting her. Trying to get in her head, and she wasn't going to let him do that.

Why had she mentioned Daisey? She should have kept that to herself.

She felt her father's hand on her shoulder. "Just be careful. He might seem domesticated, but my sources say he can be just as dangerous as Quell."

"I always look after myself like you raised me to," she said, taking the tray that the bartender had given her to carry back all the drinks. Then, smiling at her dad, she blew him a kiss before walking back to the table.

But his words lingered in her mind.

Nolan wasn't domesticated.

So what?

She wasn't planning to do anything except help him get a leg up on the competition. She knew her motives were, well…even in her own head she couldn't say pure. But they were good. Malcolm had gotten away with his underhanded business dealings for too long.

A good man like Nolan deserved a chance to get ahead. That was all she was doing, she reminded herself. Leveling the playing field. But when she got to the table and Nolan took the tray from her and Daisey hopped down from her chair to hug Delaney's legs, she knew that wasn't true.

"Come on, Daddy. We can all go dance now," she said, grabbing Nolan's hand and leading the three of them to the dance floor.

The song "Happy" by Pharrell was playing, and she tipped her head toward Nolan.

"It's her favorite song," he explained.

"Mine too," Delaney said to Daisey.

The little girl clapped her hands and then started dancing around them. Nolan had some nice moves and Delaney realized she was staring at him and made herself look at his daughter instead. Taking Daisey's hands in hers, they danced together, swirling their skirts and laughing and singing to the music.

Nolan scooped his daughter up in his arms as the song ended and a slower ballad came on. "Unforgettable" by Nat King Cole. She stood there watching the two of them dance and knew that despite what she wanted to believe, seeing Nolan and Daisey together was doing something to her emotions. It was a longing for something she'd never have.

* * *

Daisey wrapped her little arms around his neck while they danced, and then he turned and saw Delaney standing there watching them. The wistful look on her face touched him, but he knew better than to buy into her poor little rich girl persona. She'd never been someone to be pitied, and he wasn't about to start.

But there was an alluring sexiness to her beauty he couldn't deny even though he planned to ignore it. She had a way of eliciting more emotions than he had expected a scandal-prone heiress to stir in him.

"Delaney's all alone," Daisey said.

"Should we ask her to dance with us?" he asked his daughter. When he looked down into her big eyes so like her mother's, sometimes it hurt. He always did his best by her, but there were many times when he knew he failed. He was driven and worked long hours; he couldn't stop that. But he tried to make their time together special.

"Yes!"

He turned to invite Delaney to join them, but she was gone. He scanned the crowd and noticed she'd returned to their table and was on her phone. Well, that was that.

"Did she leave?" Daisey asked, disappointed.

"She's back at our table, taking a call. Don't get attached to her, Pip. I doubt we will see her again," he warned his daughter.

"But Thom's mommy said she was going to work with you," Daisey said.

"Work, not hang out with us," he cautioned.

Daisey squirmed to get down, and he set her on her feet. "Why not?"

He took her hand and led her off the dance floor to a quiet area away from the crowds. He squatted down until they were eye level. "Because she's going to work for me, okay?"

"No."

Say what? Daisey sure had her stubborn side. But rather than chiding her, he just hugged her close.

She hugged him back. "Do you think she doesn't like kids like Pamela?"

He pulled back and looked down at his daughter. "No, I don't think that. Why would you say that about Pamela?"

"She told the man on the other side of you that she didn't."

A muscle ticked in his jaw. He wished he'd heard that. But it explained a lot. "She's used to being the child."

Daisey started laughing. "Daddy, you're so silly! If Delaney likes kids, why can't we see her again?"

"It's complicated, Pip."

"You say that when you don't want to do it."

"Sometimes. But this time it's the truth. Let's go finish our cake," he said.

He stood up and held his hand down to her, and she took it. They made their way back to their table and Delaney was still sitting there, sipping her champagne and no longer on the phone. He pulled out Daisey's chair and seated her before seating himself.

"Nice dance?"

"It was," he said. "We wanted to ask you to join us…"

"You did?" she asked, seeming surprised.

"Yes," Daisey said, leaning around him to talk to Delaney. "Do you want to see us again after the wedding?"

"Daisey," he said sternly. "We talked about this."

"What did you say?" Delaney asked him.

"That it's complicated," Daisey chimed in.

"That's true," Delaney said. "What did you have in mind?" she asked his daughter. "I'll let you know if I can join you."

Daisey looked up at him. He knew she hadn't thought that far ahead. It was clear to him that Delaney didn't have many children in her life.

"Daddy and I are having a fairy hunt on Thursday night," she said.

"A *fairy hunt*?"

He nodded. "Yes. We think that there might be fairies hiding in the wildflowers in our backyard."

"Daddy and I are going to look for them at twilight," she explained.

"That's the plan," he said. He knew that the fireflies would be out then and thought they'd satisfy Daisey's imagination. He also suspected that Delaney was going to say no to joining them. Fairy hunts didn't make the society pages where Delaney lived. Which suited him just fine. He really didn't want to get to know her any better.

What he knew so far, he was intrigued by despite the fact that he wasn't too sure he could trust her. All he knew for certain was that he was noticing far too much about her.

Like her beautiful blue-gray eyes, long, graceful neck and the way that sparkly pendant rested just above the lush upper curves of her breasts. *Fairy hunt, Cooper. Get your head back in the game and away from the seductive qualities of Delaney Alexander.*

"Oooh, that sounds like my kind of fun! What time should I be there?" she asked.

From what he'd read of her, this sounded the exact opposite of Delaney's usual kind of fun. Which made him suspicious. Why in the hell would she agree to come?

"Daddy?" Daisey asked.

"I'll sort it out, Pip. Why don't you finish your cake?"

She turned back to her plate, and a few minutes later Thom and his parents came back. Once he was sure that she was engrossed in her own conversation, he put his arm on the back of Delaney's chair and leaned in so that Daisey couldn't overhear them.

"What are you up to?"

"What do you mean?" she asked, licking her lips.

Drawing his eyes to her mouth. Her totally *kissable* mouth with a full lower lip and cupid's bow top one. The way she gave him that slight smile, lips parted so all he could do was stare at her mouth, obsessed with how it would taste under his.

She tipped her head to the side and lifted both eyebrows, and he realized he was staring. "A fairy hunt sounds like your kind of fun?"

She blinked up at him, all guileless, and for a nano-second he almost fell for it. "Why wouldn't it be?"

"Lady, I don't know what you're up to—"

"I remember being six and I like fairies too," she interrupted him, but her tone was quiet and wistful. "I think going on a fairy hunt will be fun. But if you don't want me there, I'll say I have a work thing or something."

He wasn't sure what he wanted. This close to her, he could smell her flowery perfume, and it suited her. There was an airy quality to Delaney that seemed to fit with fairies and six-year-olds that loved them. But he was a grown man and didn't want to see his daughter get hurt.

"If you really want to come Thursday night, be at our place at six. We are having a picnic with fairy food to tempt them to come out," he said gruffly. "But after this, I think you should tell her that you are busy."

"Why?"

"If we are going to be working together then we can't…"

"Go on fairy hunts?"

He looked over at her and realized in a way she was baiting him. She had him on a knife's edge in a way that no woman had in a long time. He wasn't going to give in to her, though. And that was exactly what she was doing. *Daring* him to say they couldn't see each other. "You're a lovely, attractive woman, but if we are working together then our relationship must stay all business."

"Aww, thanks." She pursed her lips. "And *you're* a

handsome man, but I don't recall asking to date you," she said.

"You didn't have to," he said, reaching out and brushing her hand lightly with his. He saw the shiver that went through her and the way her pupils dilated at his touch. She felt this spark, as well. It was dangerous. And though Nolan never backed down from a challenge, he had Daisey to think about. Which meant when it came to a woman like Delaney, he had to be cautious.

Three

Delaney walked into Olive Hayes's office early Monday morning and plopped herself in the guest chair as her best friend and co-owner at IDG Brand Imaging finished up her phone call. She'd spent Sunday debating if she should actually go to Nolan and Daisey's house for their fairy hunt, which was going to be on Thursday night.

Apparently, that was the one night a week when Nolan got off work early, and they always spent time together. He'd texted her his address overnight. She liked that he made his daughter a priority. And another thing she liked? The way he'd looked at her and told her that she was an attractive woman. She could still feel the touch of his hand on hers and the shiver that had gone through her. She wanted him. It didn't do to pretend she was thinking about him because of the kind of dad he was.

There was just something about his big, muscly body and that blunt intelligence in his eyes. The way he'd looked at her as if he saw the real woman and not the society gal she used to keep everyone at bay.

But she had to be careful.

She was on a mission to even the odds and make sure that her ex's scheming didn't pay off. And sure, Nolan was hotness personified, but she wasn't going to let her attraction to him distract her from what needed to be done.

Speaking of which…she had the meeting later today at his offices to discuss his brand rollout. Where she was going to be all business like he'd said they needed to be. And not notice his wide, sexy mouth or think about the fact that she had wanted him to kiss her at the reception—

"How was the wedding?" Olive asked as she hung up the phone. "I wanted to text and make sure you were okay, but Dante said to let you do it on your own."

"And you actually *listened* to him?" Delaney quipped.

Dante was Olive's fiancé, and they'd just moved in together. They were in love, and Delaney loved them together.

"No. I was texting sort of on the sly, and he caught me. He pointed out that I said I was going to wait for you to reach out if you needed me… And I was, like, yeah, you're right, and he just raised one eyebrow and walked away. The nerve."

"Rude," Delaney said, but couldn't help smiling.

"So…how'd it go?"

"Actually, it went better than I expected. I actually met Nolan Cooper's daughter, and she introduced me to him."

"That's good. Is she cool?" Olive asked.

"She's six," she replied. "And super cute!"

"And…?"

Paisley Campbell, their third best friend slash business partner, walked in with a cardboard tray of coffees, and shot a glare at the two of them. "Are you both talking about the wedding without me?"

"Uh," Olive said.

"Yes. You're late," Delaney pointed out. "And we all know the reason why since tall, dark and sexy is back in town."

Paisley had been dating Jack for the last six months. They sort of lived together when he was in town; he had some job that took him away for weeks at a time. But he was very mysterious about what he actually did. Lately, Delaney had started to speculate that he might be a spy. He had the James Bond good looks so he could totally be.

"He is. But still you promised to wait for me," Paisley said.

"I have. I just told Olive that I met Nolan's six-year-old daughter."

"Did you know he had a kid?" Paisley asked as she handed Delaney a vanilla latte and Olive her mocha cappuccino.

"No. Did you?" she asked her friend.

"Yes. So, what happened?" Paisley asked as she perched on Olive's desk, facing her.

Delaney looked over at the only two people in the world that she was always honest with, even more so than she was with herself. These two women knew her the best and understood her flaws. Yet loved her anyway.

"Dellie?"

She sighed. "Daisey—that's his daughter—was lost and I helped her and that's how I met Nolan. Then we sat together at the reception and his assistant mentioned she wanted a meeting with me to help with their brand image rollout... Thanks for dropping my name, Paisley."

"Not a problem. So? Is he down with the whole using the info you got from Malcolm's safe scheme?" Paisley asked as she blew on her Earl Grey tea before taking a delicate sip.

"I don't know. I mean, I couldn't exactly talk about work and the aerospace government contracts with his cute daughter sitting next to us."

"Uh-oh," Olive said.

"Stop it! I'm definitely going to do it. I just haven't figured out how," Delaney said.

Olive shrugged. "Well, the total radio silence makes sense now."

"It does," Paisley agreed.

"Why?"

"A motherless child and her dad...that's complicated for you," Olive replied.

Delaney sighed and got up, walking to the plate-glass windows that overlooked Wabash below and stood there. The sidewalks were busy with people rushing to their lives, but honestly all she could see was Nolan holding Daisey in his big, muscular arms and dancing with her.

"You okay?" Paisley asked as both she and Olive came up and stood next to her.

"Dad said that Nolan might look domesticated but he's dangerous. But honestly? I didn't get that vibe from him."

Olive and Paisley both put their arms around her and group hugged her before they all went to sit on the chairs in the guest area.

"Was your dad ticked?" Olive asked.

"What did you see in Nolan?" Paisley asked at the same time.

She took Olive's question first since that was easier to answer. "Sort of. Not really as much as I expected."

"And Nolan?"

"He was… I mean, drop-dead gorgeous, funny with a blunt honesty that I liked. He's way too hot to be a single dad," she murmured.

"Wow. Okay, so what's the plan then?" Olive asked.

"It hasn't changed. Just got more complicated," she admitted. "I am trying to pretend that I'm not affected by him. Any advice on how to do that would be welcomed."

Olive and Paisley both started laughing and shook their heads. Then Olive pursed her lips. "When I was trying to deny I was attracted to Dante, I just went in all professional and then tried to keep my focus there."

"I'll try that."

"Yeah, focus on the plan," Paisley concurred. "Go in there today and get to know the brand and drop your information."

"Yes. That makes the most sense."

"It does," Olive said. "And that way you won't have to worry about the super-sexy thing."

Delaney didn't say anything, just stared down at the top of her to-go coffee cup and wondered if attending Daisey's fairy hunt was too personal.

"Dellie."

She looked over at Olive and saw concern in her friend's brown eyes. "I might have agreed to go on a fairy hunt on Thursday evening."

Paisley just stared at her and Olive looked sympathetic. "How were you going to say no to that?"

"I know, right? I mean, if I handle the information I have correctly, he'll think it was his idea and never know."

"Never know? Do you even *hear* yourself?" Paisley asked. "You're attracted to him, he is a single dad and he's the only one who can make Malcolm pay for his sneaky underhandedness. There isn't another aerospace company in the Midwest that is even close to being in Nolan's league."

Delaney stood up and shook her head. "Yes. I know it sounds crazy. I was going to say no. But Daisey asked me, and there was something that reminded me of…"

"You. We get it," Olive said. "We just don't want to see you get hurt."

Paisley took a deep breath. "Be careful, Dellie. Remember he's not the reason you are doing this. Evening the odds and making sure Malcolm doesn't get away with breaking the law is the primary goal."

"We were outbid *again*?" Nolan asked his head of contracts. "By Quell Aerospace?"

"Yes," she said. "I've asked for a breakdown of the proposals because there is no way they can beat us on cost. Or to be honest on expertise."

Nolan shoved a hand through his hair. "I agree. Do you think there is anything fishy going on?"

"I don't know. I have a friend who works on a congressional subcommittee for defense contracts, but they don't assign contracts. I could ask, but I doubt we'd get any real information."

"Thanks, Lynn. I appreciate all of your hard work. How are we on the other contract proposals?" he asked. "Most are just extensions of our current contracts, right?"

"Yes. And we have one new one that I think we can definitely win. For one thing we are the leaders in that area."

"Okay, keep me posted. I'm meeting with a private space agency later in the week. I think it's time to explore other options," he said.

"Away from government contracts?" she asked, sounding as surprised as he expected.

"Yes. I want to shake the government up and let them know we aren't dancing on their string," Nolan said. He was tired of this nonsense with their proposals, and while it might just be hard feelings from losing, he couldn't shake the feeling that it might be something more.

"I'll reach out and talk to my contacts and see what I can find out about the private market. There will be a lot more profit in it," she said, eyes lighting up.

"Music to my ears," he murmured.

Lynn left his office a few minutes later, and he opened the email file that his assistant, Perri, had dropped on his desktop. IDG Brand Imaging.

Delaney's company.

He rubbed the back of his neck. He'd thought about calling her on Sunday and canceling the Thursday night thing, but Daisey had spent most of the day in her playroom drawing pictures of the three of them on the fairy hunt. And he didn't have the heart to disappoint his daughter. So, in the end he had just decided they'd get through Thursday and that would be the end of that.

Nevertheless, he knew he couldn't hire Delaney to work with him. He wasn't going to deny that the other reason he hadn't canceled was that he wanted to see her again. Truth was, he hadn't been able to sleep when he'd gotten home from the wedding reception for thinking about her mouth.

Her lips were perfectly bow shaped and looked just right for kissing. Not little pecks on the cheek but deep, slow kisses that would inevitably lead to *more*. Nolan felt his body tighten at the thought of what he wanted to do with this woman. In fact, he hadn't been able to shake that image of her naked in his arms all night, which had made for a long, hot, sleepless night for him.

But his fantasies were never going to become a reality.

His daughter wanted her as a friend. Which put her in the no sex zone. Even if working together could be fudged, Daisey's feelings couldn't. He wasn't going to kiss Delaney. End of story.

"Sir?"

"Yes, Perri?"

"I just asked if you wanted me to set up the conference room for your meeting with Delaney Alexander or just meet in here?" she asked.

"Conference room. I think we should have Hal Stevens from Marketing and maybe Quinn Allen or someone from his team in there, as well," he said. Marketing and Finance would be keys to whether they could hire this outside team. The feedback on the previous contract they'd lost—not the one they learned about today—was that the government wanted to go with someone who had the name recognition behind them. Convincing people to move to another planet somehow was going to be easier if the public saw them as a brand they knew and trusted.

Nolan thought their safety record and the fact that he had triple-checked everything before they built it would be enough, but apparently not.

"Okay. Should I order up a tray of snacks and drinks?" she asked.

"Yes," he said, knowing he wanted Delaney to be impressed by him and the company he had made from scratch. A part of him wanted to be more blasé about her opinion of him, but she was on his mind all the time and no matter how wrong it was, he wanted to be on hers, too. He wanted her to see his success be as conflicted as he was.

His phone rang and he glanced at Perri for a moment, but she just waved and walked out of his office.

Nolan spent the rest of the morning on the phone focusing on business. Every time his mind drifted to Delaney, or he started to check the time, he directed his thoughts elsewhere. He wasn't counting down the minutes until she was in his building or anything.

Yeah, right.

When his assistant messaged him that Delaney was here, he left his office and went out to meet her.

"Ms. Alexander, it's good to see you again," he said, holding out his hand.

She raised both eyebrows at him. She wore a flowy navy blue dress with buttons down the front and cap sleeves. The scoop neckline drew his eye to her cleavage, which he forced himself to ignore. "Mr. Cooper. Are we not on a first name basis anymore?"

"I figured we should keep things more formal since this is business," he told her. He always liked to keep things professional whenever possible.

"Okay then. Let me give you this before anyone else sees it," she said, handing him a canvas bag.

"What's this?"

She grinned. "Some fairy wings for us. I thought we could use them to blend in and not scare them away. I think they should fit," Delaney said. "Is there a rest room I could use before we get started?"

"Down the hall, first door on the left."

She turned, and his assistant just cleared her throat and he handed her the bag. "Put that in my office. When Ms. Alexander comes back, please direct her to the conference room."

"Sure thing, boss."

He ignored her knowing smirk as he walked toward the conference room. Dammit! Everything he did with Delaney backfired. She kept him guessing just as much in this environment as she had at the wedding reception. He wanted to be ticked off about that but instead he was enchanted.

The first thing he noticed when she walked into the conference room was her mouth and the fact that she'd put on some kind of shimmery lip gloss. He couldn't tear his eyes from her lips. His own mouth felt dry, and he realized that not kissing her was going to be harder than he'd expected.

Delaney could tell that Nolan was trying to establish some boundaries, and she knew she should respect them. Of course, she was going to, but at the same time, whenever she made eye contact with him her mind kind of drifted into fantasy land… Exactly where it *wasn't* supposed to go. She asked for some water just to give herself a strong talking too before she got back on track with the presentation.

No matter what, she couldn't allow herself to become distracted.

She needed Nolan more than he could ever know, and she had to do her best to make sure this business deal for the company went off without a hitch. But that was part of the problem. She could use a company of this caliber to get revenge on Malcolm, but she couldn't use Daisey's dad in the process.

In her mind that made perfect sense. The relationship had to be forged in this conference room. And that was what she intended to do. She decided after she took a long swallow of water, she'd just look at the other two people in the room instead of Nolan.

"IDG Brand Management is really the only team you'll need for anything that comes up during your rollout. We specialize in handling all prongs of media and social media impact."

The Marketing guy looked bored, which made her smile. "I'm sure you're wondering why you'd need me when you have a marketing department that manages that already."

"I am," Nolan said, his deep voice resonating in the room.

"Well, what we do is more tuned to your perception. We're not helping you sell a product per se but more focused on convincing the public to embrace you to see you as someone they want to go into space with and colonize a planet with," she explained. "I know that is a big reach, but I think we can start small and build upon it, working with Marketing every step of the way."

"What do you think, Hal?"

"What do you have in mind?" Hal, the Marketing guy, queried her.

"Glad you asked. I was thinking of partnering with one of the bigger toy manufacturers to either make a model, or even better, some kind of play tent or structure of your Mars living quarters. This would be twofold in that kids can learn about the Mars environment and their parents can see some of the spaces you are creating. Also, by having it in their homes they will trust you as the provider for the Mars living pods."

Nolan crossed his arms over his big chest, making the muscles in his arms bulge, which she wasn't supposed to be noticing so she turned to Hal and the other guy whose name she couldn't remember. "What do you think?"

"I like it, but we're years away from sending families to Mars. And we need market exposure now."

"Which is why kids are the first part of the project," she said. "You want the kids who grew up playing in your Mars Pods—just testing that out as a name," she said with a wink, "to feel safe buying your Pods on Mars when they get there."

She fielded more questions about her toy idea, which she'd brainstormed with Paisley and Olive earlier in the day.

"That's more of my long-term idea. I think in the short term, we need to get to know Nolan Cooper so that Cooper Aeronautical has a face the public knows. Part of why Elon Musk is thought of so favorably is that people know him."

"I'm not Elon Musk," Nolan stated.

"Not yet," Delaney said. "However, we would start raising your profile in your industry but also with the public. Get you to be the expert the news programs and media outlets call when they are talking about space. Whatever it is, we want you to be their first call."

"How would you do that?"

"Well, I'd have to spend some time getting to know you better and figure out the right way to plan your profile, but once I figure you out it'll be easy."

"Are you saying you think I'll be easy?"

She shook her head. "Mr. Cooper, *nothing* about you is easy."

That made the others in the room laugh, and she realized she had been concentrating only on Nolan again.

"Sounds like you already have him figured out," Hal said.

She smiled at them. "I'm happy to answer any other questions you have…"

The Finance guy asked about her fee, and she had the pricing sheet that Paisley had done for her to hand over to them. She answered a few more questions about possible toy manufacturers, and Nolan spoke up then.

"I'd like to have it locally made if we can. I know a lot of small companies in this area could use this kind of partnership," he said.

"Of course. I'll start making calls and draw up a list for you," she said. "Should I leave you to discuss this?"

"If you don't mind," Nolan said. "I'll see Ms. Alexander out and be back shortly."

Delaney gathered her presentation materials and shook hands with both of the other men before leaving the room with Nolan right behind her. She thought she'd done really well today, and she'd laid some ideas about the Mars living spaces, which was what Malcolm was trying to cut Nolan out of. But had that been enough to get the ball rolling?

She sure hoped so.

When they got to the end of the hall and the bank of elevators, she turned with a big smile on her face, but Nolan looked intense as he pushed the button to call the elevator.

"Is everything okay?" she asked.

"No."

That surprised her. She'd thought her presentation had gone really well. "Why not?"

He took her hand and drew her away from the elevator and away from the offices. "I wasn't planning on hiring you."

"*What?* Why not?"

He cursed under his breath and then shook his head. "I want you, Delaney. And I never mix business and pleasure."

"I do," she said, going up on her tiptoes and doing what she'd wanted to do since she'd seen him in his office.

Four

Nolan saw her leaning up and coming in for the kiss, and he was tempted, but he needed answers first. Some of the stuff she'd mentioned in their meeting was top secret, so how did she know about it?

She'd publicly broken up with Malcolm Quell, one of his biggest competitors… Was he missing something he shouldn't? Of course, his assistant had already had Delaney on the list long before he'd met her for a brand consultant. But her presentation had touched on pieces of the long-term Mars mission that she shouldn't have been privy to.

He tried to ignore that he was pissed off because he also wanted her. He hadn't been able to stop watching that mouth of hers. So, there was anger, suspicion *and* lust at play here, which was not a cocktail of emotions that he could easily handle.

He pulled her closer and turned so that she was between him and the wall. They were out of earshot of the offices on this floor, and he didn't take his eyes off Delaney, who just looked up at him with a wicked sparkle in her eyes.

She put her hand on his shoulder. "Mmm. I like it when a man takes charge."

"Then you're going to really like me," he growled. "Because I'm not a lapdog and I've never been a pushover."

"Stop trying to turn me on," she warned softly.

He couldn't accommodate that request.

Instead, he brought his mouth down hard on hers. Because right or wrong, it was what he wanted. What he'd craved since she'd looked up at him in the church. He tried to temper himself, but she tasted…like he imagined ambrosia tasted. She was sweet, spicy and addicting. He thrust his tongue deeper into her mouth and felt hers brushing over his.

Her hands on his shoulders tightened, and she lifted her body so that he felt the sweep of her breasts against his chest. Putting his arm around her waist, he drew her even closer to him, rubbing his erection against her and then realized what he was doing.

Where he was.

F—

He tore his mouth from hers and stepped back, putting his hands in his pockets and breathing deeply. She stayed where she was, her head and shoulders leaning against the wall, eyes half-closed as she gazed at him. He still wanted her. He was seconds from taking her hand and leading her into his office, stripping her naked and taking her.

No.

"Why'd you stop?" she asked breathlessly.

"We're in my offices and despite that, I'm usually more professional. And…I need some answers from you."

"I'm on the pill and don't object to your kisses," she purred. "Anything else on your mind?"

Great. Now he was just thinking of how it was only fifteen steps down the hall to his office, where he could lock the door and they'd be alone…

"Yes, there is. First and foremost, how did you know so much about the Mars missions? That information was just sent out in a request for bids from the government this morning."

She straightened from the wall, chewing her lower lip as she studied him. He realized she was trying to decide what to say. How much truth to give him.

"I don't like liars," he warned her.

"Me either," she admitted. "I might have seen some stuff when I was dating Malcolm."

"You were arrested breaking into his house almost six weeks ago. It's been a while since you were with him, or has it?" he asked. Then his eyes narrowed at her. Was she a plant? Was this how Quell had been beating him on proposals lately? Did Quell have other inside people in his office?

"I haven't seen him since our court appearance when he magnanimously dropped the charges against me."

He folded his arms across his chest. "So…how'd you get that information?"

"I can't say here. Is it possible to go to your office where we can talk privately?" she asked.

His office. The very place he'd been imagining hooking up with her. But this was business, and as much as he wanted to give in to the lust that was raging through him at this moment, he wasn't about to. He needed answers and it seemed that the Dish Soap Heiress held them.

"Sure. Let's go," he said, turning on his heel and walking to the office. He opened the door and then gestured for her to proceed him. His assistant was still on her afternoon break, so after he closed the office door, he took his phone and messaged her not to disturb him.

Nolan walked over to the large walnut desk that had been his father's when he had been growing up. He sat down behind it and gestured for her to take a seat in one of the large leather guest chairs.

Delaney sat down, looking small and delicate in the chair. It was hard to look at the woman in front of him and see a corporate spy, but he knew that looks could be deceiving.

"So…"

"Um, well, here's the thing. I might have seen some stuff when I was in Malcolm's house. I'm not sure of the legality of telling you what I saw, and I don't want you to get in trouble," she said.

He just stared at her. What the heck was she talking about? "How would I get in trouble?"

"I think Malcolm might have been privy to some of the information that you only received today. If I tell you, would that mean you have it, as well?" she asked. "I didn't realize that until a few minutes ago."

There was a lot to unload there. First, she had seen bid specs in Malcolm's house more than six weeks ago. Next, she thought if she shared the information with him, he might be in legal trouble.

"What exactly do you have?"

She gave him a very sweet smile; in fact, it was very similar to the one she'd given Daisey when they'd said goodbye at the wedding reception on Saturday night. "Just some overheard conversations. I mean I honestly thought the housing pod information was out there. That's the reason I included it in my presentation."

Delaney was walking a tightrope with the facts here. She had been honest—mostly. But the truth was more complicated than Nolan suspected, or even herself for that matter. She didn't want to do anything that could compromise his company, but she did want to level the playing field and maybe raise some questions in Nolan's mind about how Malcolm had gotten the information. Delaney sighed. She'd guessed that Malcolm was doing something underhanded, but guessing wasn't the same as knowing.

It was only Nolan's reaction that was giving her an idea of the value of the information she held. She knew she couldn't tell him or show him the documents she'd photographed in Malcolm's safe. They contained more details of the housing project for Mars than she'd revealed in her presentation. While she did believe that Cooper Aeronautical should follow the plan she'd laid out, she'd thought she was helping them in the marketplace to get a leg up, not giving them inside information.

She had to be very careful what she revealed next if she revealed anything. She wasn't here to ruin Nolan. She was going to have to either talk to her father or maybe Jones when she left here.

Nolan was looking at her as if he wasn't sure if he could believe what she'd said. And she couldn't really blame him. She told herself she'd be much more on her A game if her entire body still wasn't humming from that kiss he'd given her in the hallway.

It had been a long time since a man had kissed her like that. If *ever*. She appreciated that most of the men she dated asked permission and made sure she wanted it, but at the same time, there was something titillating about a man who took what he wanted.

"Well?" she asked.

He was letting the silence build between them, and she wasn't sure if that meant he'd believed her or if he was fixing to call her on her BS once again. She did know that if he didn't start talking, she probably would, and that could be dangerous.

She felt too out of control.

Not something that was unusual for her. But around Nolan Cooper it seemed dangerous to her. He was too wily, and there was more to him than she'd let herself see. Her father had warned her that the single dad could be trouble.

Was he her kind of trouble? Or just the kind where she ended up humiliated in the tabloids once again? Just once she wanted a man to live up to her expectations. She definitely didn't want to be in the tabloids again. She hated that. And something about Nolan made her feel like he was different. But her gut was rarely right.

"Well, what?"

"Does that answer your question?" she asked. She'd learned early on that it was better to stay on the offensive. Keep moving and keep deflecting back to her adversary. And regardless of that kiss, Nolan was definitely not on her side. She was here for a little payback; it would be so much easier to remember if her ex's fiercest competitor hadn't kissed her.

But no regrets.

"No, but since I'm dealing with you, Delaney Alexander, I sort of expected that. What else did you overhear when you were with Malcolm?"

"Uh, I don't think I should tell you. I don't want to be accused of anything else."

He arched one eyebrow and leaned back in his chair. "Do you play chess?"

"I do, why?"

"I have a feeling that you'd be a good opponent," he mused, then bent forward and made a few notes on a pad on his desk. "I think the team is excited about what you outlined, but given your connection to one of our competitors—"

"I'm not connected to him at all. I won't bring any

more ideas like that forward until you or your team share information with me," she promised.

"Fine. But I would need you to sign a nondisclosure agreement too, and I'm going to have to talk to our attorney. Government bids are highly competitive, and any hint of inappropriate information gathering could cost me. I'll be in touch in a couple of days," he said.

"I understand. Am I still invited to the fairy hunt on Thursday?" she asked.

He took a deep breath and then nodded at her. "I won't let Daisey down. But I think it should be a one-time thing. She grows attached very easily and since I'm not sure where this is going, it will be safer for us to not let that develop."

She understood where he was coming from. On every level. She needed to start looking around for a plan B in case he did cut her off completely. But she wasn't sure he would. "I completely get it. I remember being a young motherless child—"

"I get that, but Daisey isn't you. She's my daughter and I have to protect her," he said.

"I know you do. It's hard at times. I mean, Daisey has you and you seem like a really good dad, but she must need women in her life too."

"She has a very nice nanny, and my housekeeper is like a grandmother to her." A muscle ticked in his jaw. "I'm not just keeping her in a bachelor pad, you know."

"I wasn't suggesting you were," she said, realizing she'd stumbled into an area that she really knew nothing about.

"Sorry. I might be a little sensitive about this. My

in-laws didn't think I'd be able to raise Daisey on my own, and it took some convincing for them to see that she's my world," he admitted. "And I'll do anything to protect what is mine."

She wished for a moment that she had someone in her life who looked after her the way that Nolan looked after Daisey. Delaney had always been strong enough to protect herself, but it would be nice to occasionally not have to.

"I can see that. I will wait for your call about my proposal to be your brand consultant. Thank you for a very interesting meeting, Nolan," she said, standing up and holding out her hand to him.

He stood up as well and instead of reaching across his desk, came around to stand next to her. She looked up at him as he took her hand in his and realized that she wasn't ready for this to be goodbye.

Though goodbye would be easier. Still…he kissed her like he wanted *her*. Not as the pathway into her high society world or a connection to her father. But like he had seen Delaney Alexander, flaws and all, and still wanted to see her naked.

And there weren't a lot of men who had treated her that way.

Delaney bit her lip. While she knew that she didn't always get *everything* she wanted, she mostly did, so she believed this was simply a temporary goodbye.

Nolan sat back at his desk after she left. God, that kiss had gotten to him. Big-time. He'd held on to his self-control by a thread, and honestly, his body was still pulsing and demanding more of her.

Delaney was tricky. He knew that there was an element of truth to what she'd said to him, but at the same time…was he being blindsided by lust? He didn't have a good track record when it came to women lately—hence his botched wedding date. He looked down at the photo frame on his desk that held two pictures, one of Daisey smiling up at him and the other was of him and Merri. He held her in his arms, and they both looked at the camera that they'd propped up on a pile of beach blankets at the Indiana National dunes. She'd been the one woman who he'd actually been smart about.

His soul mate who he'd planned to spend the rest of his life with. It was hard sometimes, even six years later, to deal with her loss. She'd be laughing herself silly over the situation he found himself in with Delaney. He knew that because she'd been the one person to see past the bluster that intimated most people. Well, the only person until Delaney.

"Am I making a mistake trusting her?" he asked the picture.

You make mistakes when you don't trust.

He knew the words were in his head, but they felt strong, as if Merri were here, whispering in his ear.

Nolan shook his head and got up from his desk to go back to the conference room to talk to his staff. He'd given Delaney Alexander enough time for this afternoon. He was done thinking about her.

He swore he heard Merri's laughter in his mind and ignored it.

Delaney's overheard conversation did raise an issue that he wanted to bring to his government contact, but he was going to have to figure out how to go about that. Any kind of information leak was in breech and could cost Quell his contracts with the government. Ethically he was going to have to make a complaint. But revealing his source might be tricky.

He used their company messaging system to ask his assistant to set up a meeting with his lawyers for later in the day. Then he got a text video message from Daisey showing him that she was having ice cream after school and she had some good news to tell him when he got home.

He stopped in the hallway to make a quick video to send back to her. "Can't wait to hear your news, Pip. Save some ice cream for me. Love you."

He sent the message and then pocketed his phone and went back into the conference room. His team was very enthusiastic about hiring Delaney, and Nolan knew if he wanted to dissuade his team from bringing her onboard, he was going to have to come up with a good reason, which he didn't have.

"Okay, but I am going to step back from this. Hal, you will be our liaison with IDG. I want weekly updates, and we need to have a budget that makes sense," he said. He left the team with tasks, met with his lawyers who agreed to draw up a draft of their concerns to send to the government office that handled contracts and then he was alone in his office.

He had messages to respond to, including a request for an interview, and he realized that he'd ignored what

Delaney had suggested—that he needed to raise his profile.

Damn.

He wasn't going to be able to avoid her. So that meant being chill. He could be cool with any woman he wanted. It wasn't like he was only a big raging hormone. But around her he felt like he was—she was temptation incarnate and he felt a sin coming on.

He used her business card and called her.

"Missed me already?" she asked as she answered his call.

"It's Nolan Cooper," he responded, not sure that she knew who was calling.

"I know. So, what's up?"

"What exactly would you do if you were helping to raise my profile?" he asked. "The other part of brand management was straightforward but this feels…well, different."

"That's because it is. We'd do it as a two-pronged attack. You doing more interviews and becoming the expert when it comes to talking about Mars and the long-term space missions. And then, of course, Cooper Aeronautical's online presence would increase, as well. Maybe using some of your history. I've been reading the information that Hal gave me. I didn't realize that your father had been a test pilot. Maybe we talk about his legacy if you are comfortable."

He was taking notes and listening to what she said and trying to marry it to the images of Delaney he had. Right now, in this moment, this woman was professional and intelligent, not seductive or ethereal at all. "Who are you really?"

"What do you mean?"

"Just that this woman is one I can work with. You're not flirting with me and always half-answering my questions…" He trailed off, not sure what he wanted her to say or even what he was asking.

"I'm a bit of both. I know I was coming on a bit strong, but I like you. I wanted to see if you like me too. I mean, the last time I thought a guy was into me, he totally wasn't. But I am professional, and I think I could help Cooper Aeronautical. Sorry for letting things get personal today."

Her answer was what he should have wanted to hear. It was as if she had wised up between leaving his office and going back to hers. Just lean into this and trust her, he thought. But he couldn't do that because he didn't trust himself around her.

He remembered the way she'd felt pressed against him in the hallway of his offices and wanted her back in his arms again. That possessive kiss he'd laid on her wasn't enough. He wanted her. He wasn't sure how to get that craving under control, but knew he had to.

Five

Hana Mallory's wedding to space executive Jay Park had all the subtlety of a tacky Vegas casino, but that's not the headline. Dish Soap Heiress Delaney Alexander was spotted dancing with rich and powerful single papa Nolan Cooper. I guess she's found her new victim. Cooper should watch out.

"Ugh. I swear we need to find out who this Wend-Z is and have a talk with her," Delaney said as she flopped down in the guest chair in Olive's office as soon as she got back from Cooper Aeronautical.

"Who cares what she says," Olive responded. "How'd the meeting with Cooper go?"

An image of him pressed against her with the wall at her back flashed into her mind and then the feeling of his lips on hers. Damn. That man knew how to kiss, and though that wasn't why she had sought him out, she was having a hard time remembering that.

"Dellie?"

"Huh?" She touched her lips, reliving the molten hot kiss and the longing it stirred inside her.

"Delaney Alexander."

Her name, sharp and loud, brought her head up and her thoughts back to the present. Olive was looking at her with real concern on her face, and Delaney felt bad her friend was worried about her. But the truth was, since everything had happened with Malcolm, she'd been off her game. Trying to prove he hadn't hurt her, when everyone in the free world could read in Wend-Z City's column that he had.

"Sorry. The meeting was…interesting."

"In what way? Please tell me you have given up on this crazy revenge scheme," Olive said, coming over and sitting in the guest chair next to her and putting her hand on Delaney's.

"No to revenge…but I don't really think I have it in me to be a Medici. I mean, I tried to be all cool and drop in some of the information I had picked up in Malcolm's safe, and Nolan saw through that. He asked me how I had gotten it. I told him that I'd overhead Malcolm… but I think that the scoundrel is getting inside information before his competitors get the bid specifications."

Olive shook her head. "Of course he is. There was something slimy about him from the beginning."

"I thought you said he seemed nice when we went to his Christmas party last year," Delaney pointed out.

"That was before he treated you like crap and I had

a chance to reevaluate my opinion. So, what did Cooper do?" Olive asked.

She loved that her friends always had her back. It didn't matter if she'd had no evidence of shady business dealings. Both Olive and Paisley were always going to be on her side. Her friendships with these two were the strongest relationships she had, and she knew she couldn't compromise them or the business the three of them had started to rehabilitate their own images.

"I'm not sure. I mean, he interrogated me about what I'd revealed in the meeting, but when I told him that I didn't realize it was privileged information, he sort of let it go. He liked the ideas I presented about marketing to families and children to bring up his profile. And I'm going to work on getting him on the air in some spots as an expert on travel and living on Mars."

Olive leaned back in her chair and stretched her legs out in front of her. "Good. So are you really giving up on the whole revenge thing?"

"I guess. I mean, I'm not exactly even sure how to give Nolan the damning information without putting him in jeopardy. On the other hand, I do still want to see Malcolm pay. I hate when someone cheats to get ahead."

"We all want that. Also it will give you some closure," Olive said. "This is a dilemma for sure."

Delaney blew out a sigh. "Tell me about it! But if I do abandon my original plan, what do I do with the rest of the information I have from Malcolm? I mean, I barely scraped the surface of it in my meeting today with Cooper Aeronautical."

"I think you don't mention anything else. If you do,

I have a feeling this will blow back on you. Malcolm is cagey, and if he finds out that you have it, I'm not sure he won't try to make it seem like you are the one who is actually criminal. And need I remind you that you were just in jail."

She frowned. She hadn't thought of it that way. She was after evening the odds, but if she wasn't careful, things could quickly veer out of control. Malcolm was a manipulator and had been using her to further his own agenda. Normally she was better at spotting that type of man. She still wasn't entirely sure why he'd dated her and told her he was in love with her only to break up with her a few weeks later. What purpose did that serve? She knew she had to be missing something important, but so far, she'd had no luck figuring it out.

"Okay. I'm keeping the photos."

"Good. I think you should. It will prove when you got the information and who had it," Olive said. "So Dante is talking about the holidays and going home to his family's for thanksgiving."

"Is this a big deal?"

Her friend nodded, then gave her an uneasy look. "I think his parents know who I am."

"Of course, you're in love, living together and serious. Why wouldn't they?" Delaney asked, not following what was upsetting Olive.

"They know I'm the mean girl who was a bitch to their son. I'm not sure how they are going to treat me."

"If I know Dante, then they are going to treat you decently. You're not the woman you were in college," Delaney pointed out. But she knew that it was so hard to live down a bad reputation. No matter how many good deeds they did, Olive and Delaney both were still painted by their past actions.

"You're right. Dante already told me they don't really know much but still… I wish I could go back in time and change the past."

"No, you don't," Delaney said. She'd thought about this a lot through the course of her life.

"Why not?"

"If you did, you wouldn't be the woman you are today. That means no IDG, no Dante, maybe no friendships with me and Paisley. Everything in your life made you the woman you are today, Olive. And I for one love that."

Olive leaned over and hugged her close. "I love you too, Dellie. Don't change."

She didn't seem to be able to no matter how hard she tried, she thought later when she was in her own office. She wanted to get back at Malcolm, but her heart wasn't really in it once Nolan had kissed her. Had she just been using anger to tide her over until she fell for another man? As much as she hoped not, she wasn't too sure.

Perri came into his office just before five when she was due to go home. "Boss, I'm not sure why, but Malcolm Quell's office called and wants to schedule a lunch with you in the next couple of weeks. They wouldn't give me a reason. He just wants to meet you, according to his assistant."

Malcolm Quell had had a number of chances to meet Nolan over the years. His father, Ashford Cooper, had been a test pilot along with Malcolm for Quell Aerospace back in the '80s and '90s. In fact, Nolan's dad had been working for Quell's father when his experimental spacecraft had crashed and killed him. His mom had been given a generous settlement, but no one from Quell Aerospace or the Quell family had come to the funeral. In fact, until this moment, Malcolm Quell had never tried to speak to him.

Interesting.

There was no other way to look at it. Nolan had been told today by Quell's ex that she'd overheard privileged information and now Quell wanted to meet. Nolan was pretty sure that Delaney wasn't working with Quell. There was nothing in the entire arrested for trespassing scandal that seemed like a logical setup.

But having met Delaney, he also knew that logic tended to go out the window around her. He might start out planning for their encounters to be purely professional but then he found himself thinking about the kiss they'd shared, which led to him playing out their meeting in his office in a very different way. One where they were both naked and having hot, carnal sex on his desk. Which had made for some awkward at work moments. His control seemed to have vanished when he thought of her.

"Sure, set it up. But do it at my club and make sure that I have an appointment right after so it can't drag on," Nolan said.

"Will do. That's it for business. I wanted to remind you that tomorrow is book day at school. Thom is going as Harry Potter," Perri said.

"Daisey insisted on Madeline this year. She and I went shopping for her costume last week. But thanks for the heads-up."

Perri just smiled at him. "Anytime. I'll see you tomorrow unless you need anything else?"

"I'm good. Have a great night," he told her as she left his office.

Nolan leaned back in his chair, turning to face the windows that looked out over the Chicago River. He'd worked hard to get his business off the ground and had always in his head been aiming to take down Quell Aerospace, but the last three years it hadn't really been big enough. This bid proposal they'd lost was the first one where he'd been a direct competitor and of course they'd lost.

He didn't know if he'd missed something on his end or if there was something else going on as Delaney had sort of intimated.

And then there was Delaney...

He shouldn't have kissed her in the hall. Because now he couldn't stop thinking about how she'd felt in his arms. Her lips had been soft too, but not too soft. She'd held on to him as he'd kissed her and had pulled him closer as if she wanted more.

He'd wanted more.

Hell, he still wanted her.

It should matter that he couldn't exactly trust her, but it didn't. Or that she might be in league with Quell. But again, he didn't care. He wanted her in his bed.

Plain and simple.

He heard the sound of Perri's laughter and shook his

head. He had one more meeting, and then he'd head home too. His meeting went a little long, and Daisey had texted him twice to remind him he promised to read to her tonight before she went to sleep. His business finally ended and he hurried home, getting into the house as his phone rang.

He glanced and saw it was Daisey. He put his phone on the counter and yelled up to her.

"I'm here."

He heard the sound of her running down the hall, and then she launched herself into his arms and he hugged her close.

"Mrs. Hobbs wanted me to go to bed," Daisey said, pouting. "But you promised."

"I did promise, but the next time you should listen to Mrs. Hobbs," Nolan told her as he set Daisey on her feet. "Go get the book ready and I'll be right up. Where is Mrs. Hobbs?"

"Right here, sir."

Mrs. Hobbs was his housekeeper. Daisey's nanny, Flo, had night school on Mondays this semester, so the housekeeper had been helping him out. "I'm sorry I'm late."

"It's fine. I just know that she's supposed to be in bed by nine."

"Thank you for that. I've got it from here," he told her.

"Good night, then," Mrs. Hobbs said.

She lived with her husband in a guesthouse in the back of their property. Her husband handled the lawn and garden for him, and Nolan was grateful to have them both on staff.

He went up to Daisey's bedroom and saw that his daughter had lined up all of her stuffed animals and dolls at the end of her twin bed. She had his pillow from his bed next to hers and was sitting with the book next to her waiting for him.

His heart broke a little. He tried his best to keep all of his promises to her, but there were times like tonight when meetings ran long and he was late. But she was six, so he knew that didn't matter to her. She just wanted Daddy to do what he said.

He struggled with this and he wished every day that Merri was still here. She had been the glue that held them together as a couple. She would have been a great mom.

"Ready, Daddy?"

"Yes, Pip."

He toed off his shoes and settled onto her tiny bed, his daughter curling up next to him and leaning against his chest as he opened her favorite fairy-tale book and started reading. She asked him a few questions but then drifted off to sleep. He watched her sleeping for a few minutes, knowing that he'd been right to warn Delaney against agreeing to come over again.

Delaney had a restless night with her French bull-dog, Stanley. She'd ended up sleeping on the patio of her penthouse apartment that overlooked Lake Michigan, wrapped in a blanket with her dog by her side.

She was still trying to figure out how to deal with

Nolan and so far, she had no real ideas. She was pretty sure she should skip anything involving his daughter and him. She didn't need to do anything to make him more attractive to her. Right now she was already half falling for him. Which wasn't surprising…she fell in love easily and only saw the flaws in a man after.

She was late going to the office. Not that Olive or Paisley would be surprised by that, so she didn't rush, stopping to get coffees for her friends. When she got to the lobby of their building, she saw a familiar profile. That custom-tailored suit and those large shoulders she'd never miss.

"Nolan?"

"Delaney," he said, turning to face her. His eyes seemed brighter this morning than they had yesterday, and he was freshly shaved and looked well put together. Her heart beat a little bit faster, and she knew that no matter what lies she'd been telling herself the previous night she wasn't immune to him.

"Are you here to see me?" she asked.

"I am. Do you have time for me this morning?" he asked.

"I am free until ten," she said. He followed her to the elevators once she checked him into the building. She sighed inwardly. He was close behind her, and she remembered their one kiss. She wanted him to pull her into his arms and feel him pressed against her back. He didn't say anything as she showed him to her office and told him to take a seat. She went behind her desk, which was a classic Queen Anne one that she'd inherited from her grandmother.

Her desk, unlike Nolan's, had a stack of notebooks and several pens with feathers on them. She also had a photo of Stanley from the Fourth of July when he'd worn a red, white and blue bowtie.

She pulled one of her notebooks to the center of her desk and smiled at him.

"What can I help you with?"

"Where's your computer?" he responded.

"I don't use one. I just use my phone," she said.

He shook his head.

"I know my office isn't a classical setup but it works for me. What's up?" she asked.

"Malcolm Quell called to set up a meeting with me yesterday, and I need to know that you aren't working with him."

"The man who had me arrested—"

He held his hand up and she stopped talking.

"I know it seems like I'm reaching, but Quell has never contacted me before. And it seems a little suspect that the first time he did it was the day you were in my office."

She had to agree with that. What was Malcolm up to? "I am definitely not working with him. In fact, I'd like to work *against* him. But you are right to suspect him."

Nolan shook his head. "Why?"

"Just based on that conversation I overheard and what you said about just getting the information," she said. "Also, he broke up with me in a very public way so of course I want to see him knocked down a peg or two." Delaney wasn't sure if she believed her or not and had no way of proving it without showing him the photos she'd taken at Malcolm's mansion. Which she knew she couldn't do.

She hoped she hadn't brought any trouble via Malcolm to Nolan. But they had already been competitors before she'd met him at Hana's wedding. So Malcolm had to have already been aware of him.

So why wait until now to contact him? What was he up to?

Nolan leaned forward, putting his elbows on his knees, and stared across her desk at her. "I'm asking you for the truth, Delaney. I won't ask again. What do you know about Malcolm Quell that you aren't telling me?"

His gaze was intense, and she had that wild, out-of-control feeling that she got whenever someone tried to make her do something. She didn't like it from him no matter how much she actually liked him.

Delaney tipped her head to the side, studying him, and then decided that she couldn't lay all her cards on the table. Not yet. After all, she hardly knew him. He'd kissed her, he had a cute kid, and he was Malcolm's competitor. That was it. That was all she knew about this man.

She had such poor instincts when it came to letting her guard down. "I don't know what I've done to make you think I'm lying to you. I've already answered your questions, so if you aren't satisfied, I'm sorry. If you don't have anything else, I need to get ready for my ten o'clock."

He gave her a shrewd look that made her feel as if he could see straight through her. She tried to keep her shoulders straight and her expression serene. Which was not easy. He was trying to be stern with her, and she doubted he'd expect her to be turned on right now, but she was.

"I don't know why I thought this would work. Can I trust you?" he asked.

This was a no-brainer. "Yes. I'm not trying to do anything to hurt you."

"But you are trying to hurt someone else?" he asked.

"I just told you I want a level playing field. No one should get an advantage. But am I doing anything illegal about it? No. I didn't seek out your company, your assistant called me. That's it. That's the truth as far as myself and Quell Aerospace is concerned."

He just continued to look at her and she stared back at him. She'd had a lifetime of strong, dictatorial men trying to figure out what she was thinking, and so far not one had ever come close.

That disappointed her a little because she'd hoped Nolan was different. But other than kissing her and making her lose her mind for a few minutes, he seemed to be no different from the rest.

Six

Dua Lipa was singing about walking away in her air pods as Delaney Alexander entered the offices of Cooper Aeronautical. She'd had a good morning so far, with a walk with her French bulldog along the shores of Lake Michigan and then a smoothie that was good for her and tasted delicious. Actually, she felt like it was going to be a good day.

Her phone pinged with an alert, and she paused Dua to glance down at the screen. Two notifications had come in simultaneously. One from Wend-Z City and one about Quell Aerospace.

She ignored the gossip site even though she suspected the headline was about her since she only got the alerts when she was mentioned. Today was a good day, and she would not let anything ruin it.

The Quell Aerospace alert was interesting. Malcolm had held a press conference the night before talking about Quell's next phase in the Mars landings and first concepts for habitation. She clicked on the attached video.

"We are pretty much the only game in town when it comes to experience and know-how. Sure there are other small-time players who are trying to build on the legacy of the past like Cooper Aeronautical, but they have yet to really prove themselves in the marketplace. I think everyone will feel safer living in a space designed, developed and deployed by Quell Aerospace, the first name in space innovation. End of questions."

She turned off the video and went to the reception desk to get her badge. She wondered if Nolan had seen the video. While she waited, she texted one of her contacts at one of the museums in Chicago who she knew was looking for someone to sponsor a new children's exhibit. And though she hadn't mentioned it to Nolan yet, she floated the idea of a space themed area sponsored by Cooper Aeronautical. Her friend loved the idea and had to run it past her bosses. Delaney texted back a thumbs-up. As soon as she entered the conference room, she had her answer about the video. Nolan was waiting along with Hal from Marketing, and they seemed to be involved in a heavy discussion.

Damn, the man looked good in a suit. He had that same serious demeanor that he always did, but there was something about him that set off little fires in her. Passion aside, she wasn't sure what to expect from him. Delaney knew he was uneasy about her connection to

Quell, so she needed to prove herself to him. She wanted to make him see that she was a good person. Like, when had that ever mattered? Never, but with Nolan she wanted it to.

"Hiya, boys, I guess you saw Malcolm's press conference."

"Morning, Delaney. Yes, we saw it," Hal said.

Nolan's jaw was tight, and he just looked over at her as if he wasn't sure what she was doing here. She could see the anger radiating off him, and she realized that he needed a way to channel that into action. She'd done it so many times throughout her life, first with her father and relatives and then with breakups and bad press.

"I have an idea," she began.

"Do you? Let's hear it," he said. "My idea of calling him out apparently isn't a good one."

"No, it's not. So we need you to make some public statements to counter what Malcolm said."

"Like what? I'm not a big fan of he said/he said."

"Me either. That's why I have reached out to one of my contacts at a museum. They have been looking for someone to sponsor a new children's exhibit, and I suggested you might be interested in doing a Mars-space themed one for them. They like the idea, and I think it would be good to get an announcement out today about it."

"That would be good. I don't have to do a counterpoint to Quell. I really like this idea. Hal, draft up a statement and let's get Quinn in here to talk about our charitable donations."

"I am happy to be a silent contributor if you need me

to," Delaney said. She had been planning to help sponsor the exhibit already.

"No, we'll do this on our own. Work with Hal on the statement, and we can have it ready to send out—"

"You have to go in front of the press and do it," she interrupted him. "Right now there is only one face as far as the public is concerned when it comes to Mars who isn't Elon Musk, and that's Malcolm. We need the public to see you and let them get to know the man behind Cooper Aeronautical."

"Hal?" Nolan asked, turning to his colleague.

Hal looked over at her and then back at Nolan and then down at his notes. "I think she's right."

Nolan let out an exaggerated sigh. "I hate press conferences."

"Everyone does, but we are going to get you ready, and you are going to nail it." Her phone pinged, and she glanced down to read the text from her contact at the museum. "Great news! The museum loves the idea. They need a call with you to hammer out the details. Can you do it this morning?"

"Yes. Have them call Perri. I'll get her to clear my schedule and get Finance in on the discussion," he said.

"Good. Hal, can I work with your team to make sure we have the right reporters at our press conference... and I want to get some Mars habitat mock-ups done. I'll work with my friend at the museum and then run it by you. I think we want this to feel like it's been in the works."

Nolan nodded. "Do it. You can use my assistant as

a resource, and she'll help you get to the right people here."

He left the room and she sat down ready to work. Her gut had been right. This was going to be a very good day. Beating Malcolm at his own game in the press would be more than a feather in her cap. It would be the first step toward making Nolan see she was as good as her word about helping him.

Nolan spent the morning hammering out the details of his donation to the museum, and as he hung up the phone felt unnerved by how easy it had been to set this up. He asked Perri to see if Delaney was free for lunch with him because he wanted to know more about how she'd pulled this together.

He had sent his concerns about Quell Aerospace to the government office that handled the bidding for the space missions and had received an acknowledgment that they would look into it. But that didn't really assuage his doubts about Delaney.

It was convenient, them meeting at Hana's wedding, and though he could see some legitimate connections for her to be there at the same time, her intricate knowledge of the space program he was working on made him uneasy.

"Hey, boss, she said she can meet you for lunch and suggested a restaurant that's halfway between your office and hers. I went ahead and booked a reservation for the two of you. You have about twenty minutes until you have to leave," Perri said.

"Thanks. Ping me when it's time," he said.

"Sure thing, boss." She winked, then left the office.

Nolan smiled despite himself. He liked Perri, and there were times when he found it too easy to lean on her. She knew when to draw the line. He admitted he didn't like not having all the facts. But lunch should help him get closer to figuring out Delaney.

The board had suggested hiring her precisely for the type of action she'd taken today. But Nolan wasn't sure he liked how easily she knew how to manipulate the media and the public. She was no stranger to seeing her name in the press, and he had wondered how she'd bridge the gap between her gossip girl life and real business practices. But despite his doubts, he was impressed. He wasn't going to deny that. However, there was also a part of him that was skeptical of how easily she'd pulled it off.

He glanced at Merri's picture and then leaned down, resting his chin on his fists, as he stared into her eyes. But it wasn't her. Merri was gone, and he'd been rolling through life as a single dad and workaholic businessman until…Delaney. He'd kissed her in the hall, she was disrupting his sleep and making him want her. So he knew why he wanted to figure her out.

He'd never been attracted to bad girls. He liked his women caring, sophisticated and with a good sense of humor. So what was his body sensing that his mind was missing? Oh, he knew what his body was reacting to. It was hard to miss the innate sensuality in Delaney's moves and in her gorgeous eyes. She just was a woman who embraced passion on all levels. There was no two ways about it.

And he was a man who only managed his passions by taming them into submission. Somehow, as much as it turned him on to think of taming Delaney, he was pretty sure that wasn't going to happen. She didn't strike him as the type of person to bend to anyone's will.

His phone pinged and he shut off the alarm, standing and leaving his office. He had to wonder if he was giving her too much power regarding the effect she had over him. He mulled that over during the short drive to the restaurant, but still hadn't come to any definitive conclusions by the time he arrived.

After valet parking, he entered the restaurant, gave his name to the maître d' and was seen to his table where Delaney waited.

She smiled and waved when she saw him, and he felt something. An emotion he was going to ignore because he didn't want to be happy to see her. She wasn't the kind of woman who was anything more than fun. Her track record was clear in the string of men she left behind her in life and on the pages of the tabloids.

Her arriving before him had surprised him. He had the feeling she was the type of woman who usually wasn't on time, but perhaps that was another assumption he'd wrongly made. He had to stop expecting her to be the Dish Soap Heiress and instead see her as Delaney Alexander, brand management expert.

That was all.

Never mind that she'd reapplied that shiny lip gloss that she'd worn at the wedding and now he couldn't take his eyes off her mouth. His own lips tingled slightly remembering the feel of hers under his. The way she'd felt between him and the wall. He almost groaned.

It would be easy to play this off as him not getting laid in a while, but the truth was, he saw beautiful women all the time and he didn't react like this. So these feelings must be tied to Delaney no matter how ill-conceived the attraction might be.

He was drawn to her whether he trusted her or not.

Delaney was feeling good. Her meetings at Cooper had gone well, and by the end of the day Malcolm was going to look like the big windbag he was. Nolan was looking...well, not as pleased with her as he should. Did he not realize how she'd saved his fine-looking ass today?

It was so hard not to notice how good he looked in a suit. Normally, she preferred a more fashion forward, edgy look on a man, but Nolan was pushing all the right buttons in his navy Hugo Boss suit.

They ordered lunch, and she got a mock mojito after Nolan raised an eyebrow when she suggested they split a bottle of champagne. "I'm very happy with the results of today."

"Yeah, about that..."

"What about it?" she asked.

"How did you pull together all of this so quicky?"

"It's sort of what I do," she said. "As I mentioned earlier, crisis management is my specialty at IDG. Most of the time the media want a story, and I know how to give them one that has juice and focuses on the message my clients want."

"So this isn't the first time you've done this?" he asked, seeming a bit surprised. "I really don't pay much attention to this kind of media unless it affects my business."

"Fair enough. Most of the time people like to read about scandals affecting other people. I keep tabs on every type of 'good' event going on in the city. Right now, I'm in touch with several charities that my clients can partner with on short notice if they get caught doing something that doesn't fit with their image."

The waiter brought their drinks, and she smiled at Nolan, lifting her mock cocktail toward him. "To a successful swerve campaign."

He lifted his water glass…the man ordered water to drink with lunch. And not even sparkling water. She had to admit he had the look of someone who took care of himself, and after feeling those biceps when he'd kissed her, she wasn't complaining. But she'd sort of performed a miracle and wanted all the "Atta girls" she deserved.

"So this was an average weekday for you?"

When he put it like that, she realized he saw through her miracle to the hard work underneath. "Yes, it is. I mean, you were a lot easier to handle since you weren't caught cheating on your spouse with a younger person or doing drugs in the office while kids were in the next room. But yes, this wasn't that unusual."

"Do you ever find that you just want to let the truth about someone come out?" he asked curiously.

"Yes and no. Sometimes the problem is something that my client is struggling to get over, and I know how hard that can be. Other times, like when it's the sixth or seventh time in a few months where I'm spinning their lives, I want to let them face the consequences."

The restaurant wasn't too busy and the tables here were spaced far enough apart that conversations could be private. "Then why don't you?"

She shrugged as she thought about the way to answer him. She didn't want him to think she was a soft touch, but the truth was she could be. She was one of those people who gave a lot of second chances. "Usually a client will promise they won't do it again or they have a family who will be hurt by the fallout, and I do it for them. Kids and spouses don't deserve to be in the spotlight."

He leaned back in his chair, crossing his massive arms over his chest. "Is that how you felt growing up?"

"Yes. I mean, from the day my mom died and I inherited the dish soap fortune, the media was obsessed. My father wanted me to be perfect and not give them anything to print, but that's not me," she said, taking a sip of her drink, and as usual, when she thought of her dad it made her both sad and angry. She had never been able to please him, and though she knew she should have stopped trying, she hadn't. She wasn't sure she ever would.

"That stinks," he said.

"It does," she agreed. Their food was delivered, and Nolan had ordered a huge burger and fries for lunch and she'd ordered a salad. Dang, she wished she'd gotten a burger.

She kept staring at his plate, and he arched one eyebrow at her. "Problem?"

"Just a minor regret."

He laughed as she took a bite of salad and pretended it was satisfying.

"Why didn't you order a burger? This place makes the best in town," he said.

"Not all of us are built like you, muscleman. And I don't like to work out, so a morning walk with my French bulldog is all I do and it doesn't burn enough calories to have a burger…" she admitted.

"You look good, Delaney, don't skip the burger next time."

"You think so?"

"You know I do," he said, holding a fry out to her.

She didn't hesitate, just leaned over, and when he fed her the fry his fingers brushed her mouth. God, she wanted him. He rubbed his finger against her bottom lip and then drew his hand back.

"You know I don't kiss most women who come into my office," he said gruffly.

"But you do some of them?"

"A gentleman doesn't kiss and tell," he said.

"Gentlemen are a dying breed. Trust me, lots of guys kiss and tell." She shrugged. "That's partially how I end up on the gossip sites as often as I do."

"Well, I'm not that kind of guy," he informed her.

He wasn't. She'd known that from the moment she'd met him in the church. Nolan Cooper was the kind of solid, decent man that she'd pretty much thought didn't exist anymore. And given her client list, that made sense. But there was another part of her that found it hard to believe he was real. She'd made mistakes in the past when it came to men, but those had been learning experiences.

She was smarter now. Which meant *not* falling for the man who cut off a quarter of his burger and put it on her plate without saying a word and went back to eating.

Delaney took a bite and told herself that it was the juicy beef and brioche bun making her feel all warm inside and not the big muscly man sitting across from her.

Seven

Delaney wasn't sure what she expected when she arrived at the Coopers' house for the fairy hunt, but it wasn't Nolan and Daisey in the backyard behind the pool lying in the grass with cameras. Nolan was on the ground with an SLR digital camera with a long lens on his stomach, and Daisey was sitting on his back with a smaller camera, which she rested on the top of her father's head.

"I'll leave you here," the housekeeper, Mrs. Hobbs, said in a whisper. "If you want to try to take photos, there is a camera for you too."

Delaney had worn a maxi sundress and a pair of wedge-heel slides, which she slipped off as she dropped her sunglasses and hat on the patio table and picked up the camera that had been left for her.

She had spent the last day and a half trying to tell herself that everything she'd imagined about Nolan had been wrong. That he wasn't as interesting as she kept remembering, but she had the proof right here that was a lie.

Daisey noticed her first and turned to wave at her and then put her finger over her lips to warn Delaney to be quiet. The little girl had on a pair of overalls and a large white T-shirt, and her hair was in two braids on either side of her face. Delaney lifted the skirt of her maxi dress so she didn't trip as she tiptoed closer to the pair. She lay down next to Nolan on the grass and he lowered his camera and turned, giving her that lopsided grin of his.

"Nice to see you," he said quietly. "Mrs. Hobbs and Daisey spotted a fairy door in the tree in the back, and since it's almost twilight, we think they might appear soon."

"But we have to be quiet," Daisey said in a very loud whisper.

"I will be. This is my first fairy hunt," she whispered back to them both. "What am I looking for?"

"Sparkly lights," the six-year-old announced as she settled back into position on top of her daddy with her camera resting on his head again.

Nolan lifted his camera as well, whispering out of the side of his mouth. "Fireflies."

She smiled as she lifted her own camera, not sure how to reconcile the man who'd kissed her breathless in the hall of his office, then warned her not to lie to him about her business dealings, with *this* guy. This papa just lying on the lawn with his daughter, waiting for fairies to appear.

She knew in her deepest heart that this was special and rare. For herself she would have gladly traded her fortune for one night spent like this with her father when she was a child. But the most she'd had was an invite to sit quietly in his den doing her homework while he worked.

She pushed those unpleasant thoughts away. Her dad wasn't this kind of father. So what, right? She concentrated on the here and now, and thought she saw a firefly...um, *fairy*. She snapped a picture and heard the clicking of both Nolan's and Daisey's cameras too.

After about ten minutes, the fireflies were filling the entire yard and Daisey had given up all pretense of being calm about it. She hopped off her father's back and started to chase them. Nolan rolled to his side and then to his feet, offering Delaney his hand to help her stand.

She took it. "Are we trying to catch them?"

"We are," he said with a grin.

"Where's the bag I gave you on Monday?" she asked.

"Mrs. Hobbs put it on the table."

Delaney went and got the fairy wings out of the bag. "Daisey, put these on so the fairies will think you are one of them."

The child ran to her as Nolan went to get a bug keeper as soon as the wings were on. Moments later, Daisey was off again. Nolan had enough nets for the three of them, and Delaney had enough wings for the three of them, as well. But she couldn't imagine that Nolan was going to wear wings.

But he took them from her and put them on. They spent the next twenty minutes running around the backyard and helping Daisey catch as many as she could—which amounted to three. But she was pleased. She put them in her bug keeper and then sat talking to them while Nolan fired up the grill for dinner. Delaney went with him and poured them both a glass of wine.

"You look good in those wings," she murmured.

"I know."

She laughed at the way he said it. "This isn't your first time dressed as a fairy, is it?"

"Nope. I've also been a pirate, a prince and a ballerina boy. That's how Daisey always phrases it," he said. "I have a daughter, and she asks me for things I can easily do."

"I'm glad to hear that. I love it. I wasn't kidding. You do look good," she said.

He quirked a brow. "So how did you know to buy the wings? I didn't have a chance to ask you at the office."

"If I was hunting fairies, I figured they'd come in handy," she said.

"You know I can't figure you out, right? One minute you're this sexy, society woman, the next you're buying fairy wings, then making a polished presentation—"

"Just like you, Mr. Fairy King, tough-as-nails businessman telling me not to mess with you and then kissing my socks off."

"I can't take credit for the socks. As memory serves, you weren't wearing any," he said.

She threw her head back and laughed. She hadn't ever met anyone who could go toe-to-toe with her the way that Nolan did. He kept her guessing and followed her leaps in conversation and logic in a way that sort of enchanted her. Which was silly. He was a means to an end. That was all.

But she knew that was a lie even as the thought entered her head. He was already more than that. She didn't know what she was going to do with him. Well, actually, she had a few ideas of what she'd *like* to do with him, involving him taking off his shirt and kissing her again. But she knew she'd better nip thoughts like that in the bud or she'd be in hot water.

Nolan still wasn't too sure he trusted Delaney, but she was being a good sport listening closely to Daisey as she pointed out the differences in the fairies. Not only did Delaney play along, but she even noted things that Daisey might have missed. They were seated in the sitting area around the firepit after dinner, and he couldn't help but note how the flames bathed her features in a warm, ethereal light.

"Daddy, do you think the fairies will be okay inside my bedroom?"

"They might be, Pip, but I bet they would rather be in their own bedroom tonight," he said.

She nodded. "Will you help me set them free?"

"I'd love to," he said, putting his wineglass down. "Delaney, want to help?"

"I think you two have it covered. I brought some

fun tea sandwiches for dessert. I'll grab them while you set them free."

"A samwich isn't dessert," Daisey said.

Nolan tipped his head to the side and raised his eyebrows at his daughter. They'd been working on being polite and not saying stuff like that.

"I mean, okay," the little girl said.

"I think you'll like them. They are made on sweet bread with whipped cream and fruit," Delaney said.

"I'm sure we will love them," Nolan said, nudging his daughter when she kept looking at the ground. "Won't we, Pip?"

"Yes."

"Okay. Let's send these fairies home," he said. Daisey took his hand, skipping along beside him as he carried the bug cage and they neared the back of their garden where there was a large hedge and trees.

She stooped and looked into the clear container. "Goodbye, Misty and Fizzy and Dawn. I'll miss you. Daddy?"

He leaned down. "Good night, ladies—"

"Fizzy's a boy," Daisey pointed out.

"Ladies and *Fizzy*," he said. Then opened the lid and the fireflies flew out, disappearing into the night sky.

Daisey sighed. "Do you think Delaney will come back?"

"She's pretty busy, so probably not," he said. He didn't want his daughter to become friends with Delaney. The woman had a history of flitting from one thing to the next. She also had a hard time staying out of the gossip columns, and as intelligent as Nolan knew she was, he couldn't figure her out. So no, he wasn't going to invite her to come around his young, impressionable, caring daughter again.

"But Daddy, I like her."

"I like her too, but she's too old to be your friend," he pointed out.

"Then she can be your friend," Daisey said. "I think she'd like that."

"Why?"

"Just do," Daisey said. "Do you think dessert sam-wiches will be good?"

"I have no idea," he admitted. "But even if they are bad, be polite. Just say you're full and you can have a cookie before bed."

She giggled, and he handed her the bug keeper and lifted her up onto his shoulders for the walk back to the patio. As they got closer, he saw that Delaney stood on the edge of the patio near the pool with her face tipped up to the wind, looking at the darkening sky. The wind blew her blond hair out behind her, and she had her hands open and out to her sides.

He watched her for a minute, wildly aroused by her spellbinding beauty. But he shoved that down. He was in daddy mode. No matter how much Delaney tempted him.

Daisey squirmed to get off his shoulders, and he set her on her feet. She ran over to Delaney and took one of her hands, tipping her little face up to the wind. Nolan took his phone out and snapped a picture of the two of them. He didn't analyze why he'd done it. Just knew he wanted to remember this moment.

His society heiress and his daughter just enjoying the night.

"So where are these dessert sandwiches?" he asked.

They both turned and came back over to him. Daisey came and stood between his legs, and he lifted her onto his lap as Delaney pulled the plate toward her. He noticed that the thick brioche bread sandwiches were secured in plastic cling wrap. She removed them from the plastic, made a cut down the middle and then turned them on their side as she pulled the two halves apart.

Daisey gasped, and Nolan was surprised too to see that there was a fancy flower in the middle. He could tell it was made of strawberries, and he suspected kiwi made up the stem. The fruit was surrounded by whipped cream.

Daisey scrambled off his lap and moved closer to look at them. "Did you make 'em?"

"I did. I watched a video," she said. "Try it. It's pretty good but messy."

"I like messy," Daisey said, taking one half and trying to take a huge bite. Whipped cream came out the end and got on her hands, but she didn't mind and just kept eating.

"What about you, Nolan?" Delaney asked.

"I like messy too," he said, taking one of the sandwiches. But he meant more than this treat she'd made. He was already thinking of the messy situation that he was going to have if he didn't stop lusting after Delaney Alexander. Although he wasn't a man to deny himself, he had always thought he was smart about the relationships he'd had since Merri had died. But he was beginning to understand that those women hadn't tempted him. Not like Delaney did.

Daisey wiped her messy hands on the leg of his khakis, and he just shook his head. "Go see Mrs. Hobbs and ask her to get you ready for bed."

"Daddy!"

"Daisey, it's already past your bedtime," he said firmly. "And you need to wash up. I'll be in to say good night."

"Fine," she huffed. "Good night, Delaney. I hope you can come again."

She walked into the house without looking at him, the little scamp. He couldn't help smiling at the way she'd just done what she wanted. There was no denying his daughter was like him in that respect. He'd talk to her later.

Turning to Delaney, he asked, "You said you play chess?"

"I do, why?"

He'd always found that he learned a lot about a person based on the way they played. And he needed some answers to the mystery that was Delaney.

"Fancy a game after I put Daisey to bed?"

"Sure. You know most guys don't ask me to play *chess*," she said with a wink.

"Probably because they are scared of you," he responded.

Delaney realized quickly that Nolan was a pretty serious chess player when he led her into his den and gestured to the board and chairs that were already set up.

She glanced down and noticed that all of the pieces were not in their proper places. "Daisey play with you recently?"

"Yes. She loves the board and she doesn't like the rules of chess, so we play one round of chess and one round of Daisey's game."

"Sounds fair. We can do the same thing if you are too good for me," she said.

"I doubt I will be. You seem like a wily opponent at most things." He pulled out her chair and gestured for her to sit down.

"Do you really see me as your opponent?"

"I'm not entirely sure yet," he admitted. "You are my business rival's ex. So I'm being cautious."

"I can understand that. And then there's the whole me breaking into his place thing," she said.

"About that..."

Oh, ho. He wanted details. That wasn't good. Why had she brought that up? What was she going to say? That she broke back in to get some dirt on him and had found more than she bargained for? No, she wasn't going to admit that.

"Whoever captures the first piece can ask a question and the other will answer it. Deal?" she suggested. She played chess with her father since it was the one game he played regularly, and had on occasion beaten him. If nothing else, it would give her a few extra minutes to figure out what she was going to reveal to Nolan tonight.

"Deal. But you should know I was all-state."

"In chess? Even I know that there isn't all-state in chess," she said with a laugh.

"No, in football. Just figured I'd toss in some humble bragging to turn your head," he said.

"You don't have to brag to do that," she admitted.

He arched one eyebrow at her.

"I told you I liked you in the wings. I think it's only fair to say I like you without them too," she said.

"Noted." He flashed her a grin. "You can go first."

She moved her pawn two spaces and he moved his one. They went back and forth, and since she wanted to know more about his rivalry with Quell Aerospace, she captured a pawn first.

"Well played," he murmured.

"Why, thank you." She gave him a coy smile. "Now, I believe the first question is mine."

"It is," he agreed.

She jumped right in. "Why are you rivals with Quell Aerospace?" she asked.

"Because we both want to be the predominant provider of living space on Mars," he said. "Just healthy competition."

"Is that all there is?"

"You'll have to take another piece before I answer your question," he said, making his move and taking her pawn. "You left yourself open for that."

"I did," she admitted. "So you still want to know about me breaking into Malcolm's? Or something else?"

"I'll stick with the B and E."

She took a deep breath. She couldn't reveal the stuff she knew about Malcolm's business dealings without accidently saying too much again. "Malcolm dumped all my stuff on his front porch when we broke up. I couldn't find a bracelet my grandmother had left me, and since he wasn't answering my texts and said he was out of town, I broke in to look for it. That's it."

She hoped that satisfied Nolan. It had worked for her dad, and even Malcolm was pacified with that explanation. She'd never mentioned the safe or the fact that she'd seen the documents in it. She'd guessed that Malcolm was doing something shady to get ahead of his competition based on the secretive meetings he'd had late at night and the calls she'd overheard. But she'd been surprised to see the evidence with her own eyes.

He narrowed his eyes at her. "That's it?"

"Yup."

"I think there is something you aren't telling me," he said.

"There's definitely a lot I'm not telling you, and you're keeping things to yourself too," she pointed out.

"Am I?"

"Yes. Like the real reason for your rivalry with Quell."

He leaned back, crossing his arms over his chest. "Why do you say that?"

"Because I've been in the boardroom of Quell Aerospace, and a photo of that man is on the wall," she said, pointing to the portrait on the sideboard in among pictures of Daisey and Nolan. The man who she was only now realizing must be Nolan's father.

The famous test pilot who died piloting an experimental craft for Quell Aerospace.

"My father," he said, then stood and walked over to the portrait. "He died when I was twelve, and no one from Quell came to the funeral. I do want to beat him. It's personal to me. But then I think all business should be."

"I agree with that. That's why I started IDG with Olive and Paisley. We know that no matter how much people say it's just business, it's *never* impersonal. Everyone has a stake in it, and what better way to show the world how you feel than to use yourself in branding."

He lifted a brow. "Are you trying to sell me on your company? We've already contracted with you."

"No, just trying to distract you from thinking about losing your dad," she said. "I never knew my mom since she died hours after I was born. But sometimes, even though I've lived my entire life without her, I still miss her. And feel an emptiness when I talk about her."

He turned toward Delaney, looking down at her with that intense gaze of his. "I still can't figure you out."

"Does that matter?"

"I'm not sure yet," he said, leaning across the table, lowering his head to kiss her.

Eight

She tasted of whipped cream and summer strawberries, and though he'd told himself he wasn't going to go down this route, he no longer remembered why. The chessboard was between them so the kiss should have been restrained, but she stirred something in him that was anything but low-key.

He lifted his head and when he looked over at her, she licked her lips and wriggled her eyebrows at him.

"How do you get better at kissing each time?" she asked.

He realized that she used her words as a shield, keeping her opponent off guard and guessing. But the thing was that he wasn't sure they were opponents.

"Maybe if you win, I'll tell you," he said teasingly, leaning in closer to her. As much as he knew he had to watch himself around her, he couldn't help himself sometimes. There was the business part that made it imperative that he use caution, as well as Daisey's attachment to her. But then there was this intense attraction he felt for her that took him by surprise. Still, she was hard to get a read on and in his experience that meant that she was hiding something.

But what?

In his mind the only thing coming up was her connection to Quell Aerospace. "So you saw a portrait of my father at Quell?"

"Wow, that's a big leap in topics," she said.

"You're not the only one who can do it." He needed some answers before he let this go too far. And he wasn't going to pretend that he was unaffected by her. His skin felt too tight as arousal took control. He wanted to push the table out of the way, pull her into his arms and make filthy hot love to her on the floor of his den.

But he wasn't a boy who had no control over himself and his desires. He would have her. There was no question in his mind, but first, he needed to know what she was hiding or at least the effect of whatever it was on him, his family and his business.

"Yes, I saw your dad's portrait there," she said. "Malcolm also has a moon rock and photos of himself with every famous astronaut. There is a portrait—oil on canvas—I think of Malcolm's father with Charles Lindbergh, as well. They call it the hall of heroes."

"Hall of heroes. You'd think if my dad meant that much to them, someone would have come to his funeral."

"You'd think. But I find businessmen seldom care about the people who make them money."

"You know I'm a businessman, right?" He lifted one eyebrow at her.

She nodded and blew him a kiss. "I do. I'm not sure where you stand yet. You could be the exception that proves the rule, or you could be…"

"Just like Malcolm Quell?"

"Him or H. Baxter Alexander or hundreds of other CEOs who are so busy trying to beat the competition they lose sight of why they started."

"Am I about to get an ethics lesson from society's bad girl heiress?" he asked drolly. A little surprised at the fervor in her voice since she normally worked so hard to seem unaffected by everything and everyone around her. He liked seeing this side of her.

"No, that's it. Stepping off my soapbox."

But it was clearly a hot-button issue for her. Her quibbles weren't just with Malcolm, but with her father. Interesting. He had no idea what that meant at this moment, so he tucked that away for later.

She took her move in the game, leaving her king vulnerable and he moved to check. She quickly moved to block and the game continued in silence for a few intense minutes. It dawned on him that she was testing his defenses. Her movements seemed erratic, but she was watching carefully to see how he played.

Nolan hadn't played against someone like Delaney before, so he was tempted to abandon his normal strategy to see what would shake her up. He debated a moment if winning or knowledge was more important, and since this was only a game and he needed to figure out her motives in the real world, knowledge won as it often did with him.

He shifted his strategy, making seemingly careless mistakes to see if she would take advantage of them.

She didn't.

"What are you up to?"

"What do you mean?" he asked.

"You're not a careless player, Nolz. So why are you suddenly putting opportunity in my path?"

He wasn't someone that people called by nicknames. He was always Nolan. To his parents, coworkers, friends. The fact that she'd shortened his name in that way caught him off guard. Which was another thing she did. When things changed around her, she seemed to try to get under his skin. Was it simply so she could regain her own footing? He wasn't sure.

"You tell me, Delz."

She threw her head back and laughed. "Don't like nicknames?"

"I think you might be the first to attempt to use one with me," he admitted.

"Why is that? My friends call me Dellie, by the way," she said.

He leaned back in his chair, knowing he wasn't going to tell her that he'd always been too serious and focused on his path. He wanted to reclaim the legacy that he felt had been lost when his father died. To that end, he wanted Cooper to be the name in aerospace and on this Mars mission to honor his father. So he'd never been one to chum around at school. He focused on his studies and then college and then running the business.

"*Dellie?* So, tell me, who are your friends?" he asked.

"Olive and Paisley," she said. "They are my business partners too. They aren't into the whole party scene, so they usually aren't photographed with me."

"So they are part of your real life?" he asked. "I mean, the party scene isn't who you really are, is it?"

She tipped her head to the side and studied him for a long time. He had no idea what she was looking for, but she seemed to find it because she chewed her lower lip for a second before shrugging. "No, it's not. That's mainly to irritate my dad—yes, I know it sounds juvenile, but I can be petty."

Delaney knew that Nolan was trying to pick apart her image and find out what was real and what was for show. She was telling him bits of the truth, but she wasn't sure how much more she would give him. Because, in all honesty, she'd never really trusted any man and wasn't sure she could start now.

"It's not juvenile," he said.

His response surprised her. "Maybe not, but I doubt you'd make the same choices I have."

"Why would I? We are two different people. And your life has shaped you, Delaney. Don't sell yourself short," he told her. "But also don't take shortcuts."

"Is it your massive height that makes you focus on the diminutive?" Once again, she was deflecting. But she knew he was right. She *had* been shaped by her life. The only time her father interrupted his busy schedule for her was when she was in crisis. So she got into mischief at boarding school. Drank and did drugs to gain his attention. Slept with men she shouldn't have and did things that were labeled bad or dangerous. But it had become a habit, and it was the only time when he focused on her.

"It is. I really have a hard time with tiny things except my daughter," he said.

Yes. That was true. He had shown himself to be the kind of father that Delaney hadn't realized existed, and she was curious how he did it and why. Was it Daisey who made the difference? Was she somehow a better child than Delaney had ever been?

"You are particularly close to Daisey. Why is that?" she asked with more bluntness than she'd meant to.

"Why wouldn't I be?" he countered.

"I am just trying to understand your dynamic, that's all. On the surface you and Daisey are very similar to me and my dad and yet…very different." She huffed out a breath. "Never mind. Let's just finish this game. I need to be going soon. I left Stanley at home alone, and he is probably getting worried."

He furrowed his brow at her. "Stanley?"

"My sweet French bulldog." She shot him a sassy look. "Did you think I had a boy toy stashed at home?"

"If you did, I doubt his name would be Stanley," he said dryly.

"What's wrong with Stanley?"

"Nothing, I guess. Just doesn't give off boy toy vibes."

She couldn't help but smile. "Interesting."

"Is Stanley your first dog?"

"Yes," she said. Not sure what else to add. Her therapist had suggested she get a pet a few years ago, so she'd gone to the humane society and fallen in love with Stanley. He'd been a bit of a handful at first, but she'd taken him to training sessions and soon came to realize that her therapist had been right. Having someone to care for had forced her out of several of her destructive habits.

It had also led her to think seriously about starting a long-term relationship, which had led to her affair with Malcolm. And that hadn't ended well. Maybe she should have stuck to dogs instead of men.

"You don't strike me as the pet type," he remarked.

She had been about to move her bishop and put him in check when he said that.

"Why not?" she asked.

He shrugged, then gestured for her to move. But she didn't.

She tried to think of something positive that he could have meant when he'd said that, but it eluded her.

"Come on, spit it out. What did you mean?"

"That you just don't seem like someone who'd want to take care of a dog. I mean, it's a 24/7 job, sort of like parenting."

"Yeah, thanks for that," she said. She moved her bishop and put him in check before standing up. "One of the things that growing up with my father taught me was how not to be a good parent, so with Stanley I just do the opposite. That's check and I think mate. Good night, Nolz. It's been interesting."

Delaney turned and started to walk to the door, but

the heel of her sandal got caught in the hem of her dress and she stumbled but righted herself. She'd never been good at making a dramatic exit. But she just kept walking. The important part was to make her escape. Get out of the room before she let him see that his words had hurt her.

And why had they? He was nothing to her except a business contact. Sure, she'd thought he was different when she'd seen him with his daughter, but she could tell now that he wasn't. That there was a part of Nolan that was exactly like her father.

Which shouldn't have surprised her.

"Delaney, wait."

She ignored him and kept walking. She really wished she was the type of person who could learn something more quickly than she did. Like she had to keep being let down by men.

Nolan caught her arm, tugging her to a stop, and she jerked her arm free as she turned to face him.

"I'm sorry."

Well, she hadn't been expecting that.

He didn't guard his words, never really had, but he certainly hadn't expected her to be hurt by what he said. She seemed like the type of person who drifted through life on the surface level and now he knew she wasn't.

The look on her face told him she was well over him, and he didn't blame her. Not really. "I misjudged you."

"You did. I know that I haven't exactly been open with you, but I thought…well, tonight I guess I thought you might see a different side of me, but I'm always going to be the dish soap heiress to you, aren't I?"

Was she? In truth, he wasn't sure. He didn't trust her—he'd already decided that—but he had just admitted to misjudging her, and maybe it was time to let some of his preconceived notions go. "No. You're not. Tonight you were someone I wasn't expecting, and I guess I pushed to see what was real."

"Fair enough. I should say that I wouldn't be here if I was the woman Wend-Z City portrays me as."

"Indeed. So should we start again?" Nolan asked.

"No. Then we'd have to pretend you never kissed me and that I never rescued Daisey. Let's just try not to hurt each other," she said.

"Deal," he said.

"Just like that?" she asked.

"Well, no one likes to be hurt, do they?" Nolan asked.

"You'd think not. But there is a lot of carelessness in the world," she said.

"Your world?" he asked.

"Yes. Yours?" she countered.

"I try not to let there be, but I can't always control my tongue," he said.

"Liar," she said, turning more fully toward him and putting her hand on his chest. "You are a very controlled man."

"I like to pretend I am, but a certain blonde has a way of getting under my skin and eroded it."

"Me, perchance?" she asked, arching one eyebrow at him.

He pulled her into his arms and lowered his head,

kissing her and stopping this repartee, which wasn't doing anything but turning him on. She was quick and clever, and he couldn't help but admire that. He also hated that he'd misjudged her so badly. Nolan knew he was usually better about reading people, but to be honest, he usually didn't lust after many women he met.

Perhaps if he had her, then his judgment would snap back into place. He turned so that his back was against the door and pulled her flush against him as he lifted his head. She put one arm around his shoulders and he felt her go up on her tiptoes. He pulled her off her feet, effortlessly holding her so that she wasn't reaching to kiss him.

She touched the side of his face, tipping her head to the side to study him. He wondered what she was searching for, but the fact that she was looking at him and not kissing him was a signal he couldn't ignore.

As their eyes met, he wished he could read the emotions in her eyes. But she was still a mystery to him. "You're a very good kisser."

"So you mentioned. I'm good at a few other things, as well," he said.

"Not chess," she retorted. "But I'm willing to let you try to dazzle me."

Dazzle her. He was going to leave her breathless and exhausted and very aware that she'd been in his arms. Not wasting a single moment, he carried her across the room to the leather sofa and sat down, pulling her onto his lap. She put her arms around his shoulders, running her hand down his jaw and looking into his eyes as if she was trying to unravel him.

He was very aware that he had to be careful with Delaney. Hurting her had made him feel something that he hadn't expected. Something more than contrition and possibly regret. Regrets were something he didn't do. She didn't seem the type to do them, either. "I'm not making any promises tonight."

"I'm not asking for any," she said.

Good.

Before he could say anything else, she put her hand in the hair at the back of his neck, running her fingers through it and sending shivers down his spine. His erection stirred, and he realized that Delaney wasn't a woman who hesitated.

Which was exactly what he liked. He turned her more fully against him as he kissed her again, his hands sweeping up and down her back. He wanted to roll her under him and peel that airy dress of hers off so they could spend the rest of the night learning each other's bodies.

Clearly, she was of a similar mindset. He felt her fingers on the buttons of his shirt as he slowly pulled the hem of her dress up, his fingers dancing over the smooth skin of her calf and knee. Her fingers were light and warm against his chest. She stopped when their bodies got in the way of her unbuttoning, so she pushed the sides open and he felt her fingers on him. Then she pulled her mouth from his and gazed hungrily down at his chest.

He continued pushing the hem of her dress higher, and she had a faint smile on her lips as she lifted the gold medallion he wore to examine it more closely. It was a Saint Christopher medallion that had been his father's and that he'd been given on the day his dad died. She rubbed her finger over it.

"I'm not sure he's a saint anymore," she murmured.

"Me either. It was my dad's."

She looked up at him. It was impossible to keep emotion out of his voice now. Earlier he'd been able to pretend that he could, but now with her in his arms, he wasn't thinking about hiding.

She rubbed her thumb over the medallion and let it fall back to his chest before she shifted and finished unbuttoning his shirt. He pulled her dress up to her waist and she straddled him, rubbing her center against his erection. A primal growl rose to his throat. He cupped her butt as he thrust against her, wanting, *needing* more.

She kissed the side of his neck and then caught the lobe of his ear in her teeth. A shaft of white heat went straight down his body, hardening him even more.

"I'm ready to be dazzled."

Nine

Nolan wasn't a man to backtrack once he made up his mind, and he'd thought he could let Delaney walk out of his house without taking her in his arms. But clearly, he'd been wrong about that. She tasted like the last days of summer, a temptation to grab the last of the sunshine before it was gone. And he knew this wasn't long term.

But not everything in life had to be. In fact, the way she felt beneath his touch was the only thing he concentrated on this evening.

This need felt like obsession, something strange and powerful that was consuming him. The more he tried to put her from his mind, or make her make sense, the less she did. Conversely, that wasn't lessening his need for her. Sex was his equalizer. He figured once he'd had her, the craving would subside.

But would it?

There was something unique and special about her that was unlike any other woman who had crossed his path before. Her blond hair was long and curled around her shoulders, and as she leaned forward to caress his chest, it brushed against his naked skin. It was cool and soft; he caught a strand in his fingers and drew it up to his lips. He wanted to know every inch of her, to memorize this moment and everything about her.

Nolan had to leave nothing unexplored, had to know her inside and out if he had any shot of exorcising her from his consciousness. He looked down at his large, tanned hand against the creamy whiteness of her thigh. It was slender and soft not hard and muscly. He couldn't help but smile as he remembered her comment about not liking exercise.

"What is it?"

"You don't need to exercise. Your legs are perfect the way they are."

"Are they? So you're saying I should have more burgers?" she teased as she leaned forward, her breath warm against his skin as she spoke.

"Definitely."

He pushed his hand farther up her leg, and the light blue fabric of her dress pooled around her waist as he reached behind her to cup her butt in his hands and draw her closer to him. She shifted, and he felt her center rubbing over the ridge of his erection.

He caught his breath as he hardened even more. He wanted her.

Now.

He didn't think he was going to be able to take this

slow and easy as he'd been imagining he could. He wanted his shaft buried so deep inside her that there was no gap between where he ended and she began.

She put her hands on his face as she rested her forehead against his.

"You're making things complicated."

"Am I? I thought I was just heating them up."

"Oh, you're doing that too," she whispered. "But I told myself that I wouldn't sleep with you."

He realized that she was caught between the same lust and common sense that he was, which surprised him. "If it makes you feel any better, I'm not planning to sleep."

She chuckled. "Don't make me laugh."

"Why not?"

"It makes me like you more, and I'm not sure if that's a good idea or not," she admitted.

She might be voicing her doubts, but even as she spoke, her thumb was rubbing over his mouth and her hips were subtly rocking against him. Her body was pretty sure, he thought.

"Good idea or not, it's inevitable," he said, running his finger along the edge of her panties until he slipped it underneath, caressing her butt cheek. "Don't you agree?"

In response, she brought her mouth down on his with all the passion he had sensed teeming under the surface. She held his face in her hands as she shifted so she was above him and kissed him long and deep. Her tongue taking his mouth completely, causing him to stop thinking altogether.

Hell, he stopped doing everything but enjoying this moment and this woman who was claiming him as hers.

Hers.

Whoa.

He didn't belong to anyone. He had to change the balance of power here, but damn. She felt so good that the last thing he wanted to do was stop this. Her hips were moving more rapidly against him and he shoved his hands inside the back of her underwear to cup both of her buttocks and try to take control of her thrusts.

She didn't stop kissing him, but her hands moved down to his shoulders and he felt the bite of her nails as she held on to him and he realized that she was close to coming. Just from this kiss and a few caresses. He drove her harder against him, but he wanted more. Needed more of her.

He tore his mouth from hers. She was over him, her breaths coming hot and heavy, her lips swollen and glistening from their kiss. He pulled her dress up and over her body, and she tossed it to the side. Then he reached behind her and undid her bra with one hand.

She shrugged out of it, and he caught his breath as he saw her breasts for the first time. They were full and round and absolutely exquisite. He cupped them both, felt her nipples poking into his palms as she rotated his hands against them. She arched her back, pushing his hand off one of her breasts as she drew his head down to it.

He took her nipple into his mouth, suckling her as she continued to ride his shaft. Her hands were on the back of his head, clutching at him as if afraid he'd leave, but he couldn't. He wanted this as much as she did. Wanted her to come in his arms so he'd know what she looked like when she lost control.

He continued sucking at her breasts as she rocked harder and faster against him. Her pure, uninhibited pleasure driving him wild with desire, he drew his finger down the crack of her butt and then she shattered. She shivered and moaned, calling his name as she came.

She was throbbing all over, and as good as her orgasm felt, she still wanted more. She wanted the thick, hard length of Nolan's cock inside her. She almost groaned. Why was she always a slave to her hormones? She hadn't been joking when she said she'd promised herself she wouldn't sleep with him.

But oh, my God, Nolan. He was so big and sexy and smart, which was another big turn-on. The way he'd played chess—chess for the love of all that was holy—shouldn't have been so hot, but it had been.

And his mouth on her nipple had sent her over the edge. Now she wanted to repay the pleasure. She had unbuttoned his shirt and pushed it off his shoulders. He cursed, jostling her on his lap as she undid the buttons at the cuffs and then took it all the way off, tossing it in the same general direction as her dress.

She leaned forward to touch his big, muscled chest, which was covered in a light dusting of hair. His skin was hot and smooth under her touch, the hair soft and springy, and she kissed the pad of the muscle over his heart. His breath was warm against the back of her neck, and his finger kept moving up and down in the furrow of her butt.

She quivered as she kissed his flat nipple and he jerked his shoulders.

"I don't like that," he said.

"Fair enough. What do you like?"

"You."

She glanced up and their eyes met. His dark obsidian gaze so serious and intent that another pulse went through her core. She licked her lips and wriggled her eyebrows at him. "Good."

Then she leaned forward, exploring his torso with her lips, taking time to kiss and nibble at him until he was moving underneath her, and his erection hardened even more. She found a jagged scar on his side, and she shifted on his lap to get a closer look at it. It was probably two inches long and looked like it had been pretty deep. But it was old and had scarred over, probably healed as much as it could at this point.

"What's this?"

He craned his neck to see where she was pointing.

"Scar."

"Duh."

"I went through a…wild streak after my dad died," he told her. "I was doing some car surfing and got cocky."

"I don't—"

"I'm not talking about old dumb decisions," he said firmly, pulling her down and kissing her until she couldn't think of anything but having him inside her.

She skimmed her hands down his body and found the fastening for his pants. Undoing it and pushing her hand inside, she stroked him through the fabric of his underwear. She felt a drop of moisture at the tip of his cock then rocked back on his thighs and looked up at him.

"In case you forgot I'm on the pill if you don't have a condom," she said.

"And I'm healthy. You think of everything, don't you?"

She shrugged. "I don't want this to be a dumb decision for either of us."

Even though a part of her felt like it might be too late. She wasn't walking away from him. Because right or wrong, she wanted everything that Nolan had to give her tonight. And later it might end up hurting her, but right now she had the hope in her heart that he wasn't going to be a regret.

He canted his hips forward, keeping his hands on her hips. "There isn't anything dumb about this."

"Glad you think so," she said. She didn't want to remind him that she wasn't known for common sense but then stopped herself from that thought. Why did she always try to punish herself for something that felt good? It was like she was afraid to let herself just be happy in the moment.

Could she do it?

Just enjoy this time with Nolan and not let her world interfere?

She was going to try.

Delaney shivered delicately as he ran his hands up and down her back. She loved the feeling of his hands on her. Wanted more. She tried to free him from his underwear, but she was afraid of snapping the elastic and hurting him.

"Get your dick out."

That surprised a shout of laughter from him, and he threw his head back as he kept laughing.

"Damn, Delaney."

She couldn't help but smile at his laughter as he was freeing his erection. She liked the sound of it. Deep and rumbling but also, she suspected, a bit rusty. He was a serious man who had a lot of responsibilities, and she was very glad she'd made him laugh.

"Damn, Nolan," she said as she saw his length. He was massive, and she wasn't sure how comfortable it was going to be when he was inside her.

But she was definitely going to have him.

She balanced herself with one hand on his shoulders as she took her panties off. Once that was done, she settled back on him and felt his dick against her bare pussy. She liked it. He felt so good.

There was also the slight exoticness of the fabric of his pants against the insides of her thighs as she straddled him. His hands were all over her, drawing her to him, his mouth on hers as he caressed her up and down.

She shifted and felt the tip of him at the entrance of her body, and she tried to lower herself on him. But he didn't just slide in. Instead, he shifted her in his arms, and she felt his fingers at the entrance of her body, circling her clit until she was dripping. Then he positioned himself at her core and their eyes met as she slowly lowered herself on his cock.

She wanted to go faster, but he was so big she had to take him slowly. "God, woman, you are killing me."

"Too much?"

"Not enough."

Emboldened by his words, she brought her mouth down on his and took a deep breath as she lowered herself all the way onto him. He held her in his arms, his hands rubbing up and down her back as she adjusted to the too-full feeling of having him inside her. She took a few deep breaths and he did too.

Their eyes met and she realized she'd never felt closer to anyone than she did to Nolan at this moment.

"You take my breath away," she said.

Nolan wasn't sure he wanted to talk. She was so damn tight around him and he held on to his control by the barest of threads. Then she leaned forward, and the tips of her breasts brushed against his cheeks as she braced her hands on the back of the leather couch. He was surrounded by her scent and feel; she was all over him like a brand. Which complicated matters. He was trying to keep this just about sex, but feelings— emotions that he didn't want—were roiling around inside him.

"I was aiming to dazzle."

He turned his head and drew her beaded nipple into his mouth. Suckled her deeply as he plunged up into her body. He could feel how tight she was and used his hand on her clit to keep her aroused. He wanted her to come again while he was inside her.

"You…are…"

He built them both toward the pinnacle again. Then tipped her head toward his so he could kiss her. Her mouth opened over his and he told himself to take it slow…but he felt like if he didn't take everything she had, right here, right now, then she'd be gone and nothing would be the same again.

So he nibbled on her and held her at his mercy. Her nails dug into his shoulders and she moved forward, brushing against his chest. Her nipples were hard points and he pulled away from her mouth, glancing down to see them pushing against him.

Nolan caressed her back and spine, scraping his nails down the length of it. He followed the line of her back down the indentation above her backside.

She closed her eyes and held her breath as he fondled her, running his finger over her nipple. It was velvety compared to the satin smoothness of her breast. He swept his finger back and forth until she bit her lower lip and shifted herself on his lap.

Then she moaned a sweet sound that had him leaning up to capture her lips with his. She slanted her head to the side, allowing him access to her mouth. All the while she held his shoulders and moved on him, rubbing her center over his erection.

He pushed her back a little bit so he could see her. Her breasts were bare, nipples distended and once again begging for his mouth. He lowered his head and suckled.

Nolan held her still with a hand on the small of her back, then he buried his other hand in her hair and arched her over his arm. Both of her breasts were thrust up at him. He had a lap full of woman and he knew that he wanted Delaney to the point of insanity, yet he wasn't going to stop. He was going to take every inch of her and hope that this assuaged the need he had for her. That this one night together would be enough.

But watching her in the throes of passion *did* something to him.

Her eyes were closed, her hips moving subtly against him, and when he blew on her nipple, he saw gooseflesh spread down her body.

He loved the way she reacted to his mouth on her. But he wanted to taste *more* of her. Moving upward, he sucked on the skin at the top of her collarbone as he thrust harder and deeper into her. Nolan knew he was leaving a mark with his mouth and that pleased him. When she was alone later, he wanted her to remember this moment and what they had done together.

He kept kissing and rubbing, pinching her nipples until her hands clenched in his hair and she rocked her hips harder against his length. Then he lifted his hips, thrusting up against her.

She clutched at his shoulders as he made love to her. Holding him to her, eyes half-closed and her head tipped back.

He leaned down and caught one of her nipples in his teeth, scraping very gently. She started to tighten around him. Her hips moving faster, demanding more, but he kept the pace slow and steady.

Building the pleasure between them.

He rotated his hips to catch her pleasure point with

each thrust, and he felt her hands in his hair clenching as she threw her head back even farther.

He varied his strokes, finding a rhythm that would draw out the tension at the base of his spine. Something that would make his time in her body, wrapped in her silky limbs, last forever.

"Hold on to me tightly."

She did as he asked, and he rolled them over so that she was beneath him. He pushed her legs up against her body so that he could pound deeper.

Her hair spread out on the dark leather couch; her blue-gray eyes met his and he felt something shift inside him. But he forgot about that as she scraped her nails down his back, clutching his buttocks and drawing him in. His sac tightened and his blood roared in his ears as he felt everything in his world center on this one incredible woman.

He called her name as he came. She pulsated around him, and he looked down into her eyes as he kept thrusting. He saw her eyes widen and felt the contractions of her body around his as she was consumed by her orgasm.

Breathless moments later, she wrapped her arms around his shoulders and kissed the underside of his chin.

"This wasn't how I saw the night going," she said softly, drawing her finger over the scar on his side. "But I can't say I'm unhappy about that."

Ten

A loud scream rent the air and Nolan rolled off her, fastening his pants as he rushed from the room. She heard the cries continuing to get louder as she got dressed. Daisey seemed to have finally stopped crying, but Nolan hadn't come back and Delaney suspected he'd be gone for a while. She snuck down to Daisey's room and peeked in, noticing Nolan holding his daughter, his own eyes closed. There was a lump in her throat as she turned away. And...well, she didn't want to overstay her welcome, so she grabbed her bag and left.

The streets weren't crowded since it was nearly midnight, and as she drove, she played back the entire night in her head. She wondered if she should regret her actions but couldn't. It had felt too damn good. But Nolan was...complicated. And as much as she wanted to enjoy this feeling for as long as it lasted, reality always intruded. She knew that better than most. She had just pulled into her own garage when her phone dinged.

Delaney glanced down to see a text notification. Her heartbeat sped up as she saw it was from Nolan. She wished she'd stayed—sort of—but would have had no idea how to act because she felt vulnerable. From the sex that was more emotional than she'd expected and from seeing him in papa bear mode.

Nolan: Sorry I had to run out. I guess you went home. Thanks for tonight.

Delaney: No problem. Daisey is always the priority. I knew she'd need you and felt like going home was the best option. See you in the office tomorrow. Night.

Nolan: See you then.

She stared at the screen for a few minutes longer and then remembered the photo she'd snapped of him and Daisey. Finding it, she assigned it to his contact. She wasn't sure what had surprised her more, the sex or this guy. The dad who had gone to a lot of work to set up a fairy hunt for his daughter.

Delaney went into her house, and Stanley came running over to her. As she crouched to pet him, he went up on his back legs and began licking her face. A little while later she let him out so he could do his business. She hadn't ever admitted this to anyone, but she wanted a person to be as excited to see her as Stanley always was.

She sighed, then grabbed a glass of water and went upstairs. Stanley trotted along beside her then headed straight to his bed in the corner of her room as she showered and got ready for bed. Once she was settled between the sheets, she looked at the photos on her phone again. All the selfies she'd taken over the last few days, the photos of Daisey and Nolan, as well as the documents she'd found in Malcolm's safe.

The more she got to know the CEO of Cooper Aeronautical the more she felt like she should tell him what she'd found. But she wasn't sure how it would help. And what Nolan would think of her if he knew about the damning documents. Her conscience was clean because she believed that no one was above the law. Not even Malcolm, who used his money and influence to circumvent normal channels to get contracts for his company.

She also had seen the way he'd treated his household staff and his company employees. They deserved better. To be honest, they probably deserved a better champion than a scandal-prone heiress, but she was all they had. So she'd keep working with Nolan and helping him the only way she knew how.

Delaney jotted a few notes from the files she'd found in Malcolm's study so she would know what was safe to mention to Nolan. She wondered at all the billionaires who were trying to get off the planet—it wasn't just Malcolm or Elon Musk but also Jeff Bezos and Richard Branson who were making plans to go into outer space. Her father said it was the quest to conquer the unknown and be the first.

Was that why Nolan was going after the Mars mission so strongly? She didn't think having his name on things mattered, but he had named his company after himself, and his own father had died testing an experimental aircraft so…what did it mean?

And was she seriously lying here in the wee hours of the morning trying to find a reason not to like him? Yes. Yes, she was. Part of it was her own abysmal track record with men. The other part was there was more to him than met the eye. He was a type A alpha, workaholic and single dad. But there was more. Something she just hadn't figured out yet, and that wasn't like her.

She normally got a bead on a person within a few hours, if not by the second time they met. So why was he so perplexing? It could be because she was beginning to have genuine feelings for the man. That emotion had been in short supply since her breakup with Malcolm. Sure, she'd had a few one-night stands and done a few shocking things to mask the pain, but she hadn't let herself be truly vulnerable to anyone.

She kept coming back to how Malcolm had lied to her and maybe used her. But the truth was more complex than that. Deep down she hadn't truly ever trusted him enough to let her guard down because she hadn't ever felt that free to be herself.

Tonight, though…she came close to being who she actually was. Nolan was making her want to drop those walls she'd used to protect herself for so long, and as much as she wanted to pretend that was a good thing, she had her doubts.

Because she'd never been enough.

She'd never been worthy.

She'd never felt accepted for who she was.

What was she going to do? Stanley sleep barked and she glanced over at her tiny dog, wishing that people were as easy to figure out as animals were. But they weren't. They never would be.

And she knew that if she wanted to figure Nolan out, she had to stop pretending to be Insta-Delaney and instead had to be the *real* woman.

Nolan hadn't been surprised that Delaney was gone when he'd calmed Daisey and gone back to his den. His daughter rarely had nightmares. She'd told him she'd dreamed she'd lost him in the fairy forest and had cried out to find him.

But now he was alone. Delaney was gone. Why would she stay? And it didn't surprise him that she kept her distance from him over the next two weeks. He'd seen her fleetingly at meetings with Hal and Quinn as they went over the details of the children's exhibit at the museum and finalized their new partnership with local toy manufacturer Playtime.

He'd also glimpsed her in the society pages and on the internet gossip sites. Not that he'd started trolling for them, but Daisey usually mentioned it and eventually he had to tell her nanny to stop letting her follow Delaney. He wanted to break the bond between the two of them now before it got any deeper. In her six years,

Daisey had only had a really close attachment to one other woman and that was Perri, his assistant and the mother of her best friend.

And that one felt safe. Like Perri wasn't going to do anything to hurt Daisey. She also was married and had the kind of complete family that at times he knew Daisey missed. Most of the time she seemed okay with it just being the two of them, but there were moments when he felt how deeply she missed having a mother.

And he got that. But Delaney Alexander wasn't going to fill that emptiness in her life. Or in his.

What he and Delaney had shared was sex. That was all it could be. Plain and simple. He wasn't going to chance a relationship and have it not work out. Not with his little girl already half in love with Delaney.

Besides, Delaney hadn't indicated to him that she was looking for anything more than a fling.

As he got dressed in his tux for a charity event at the museum that evening, he told himself he wasn't taking extra care in the hopes that he'd run into Delaney. She had set out a plan to raise his image but it didn't necessarily include her in all of the events.

"Daddy? Why are you staring at yourself?" Daisey asked from her spot in his closet where she was seated on the large, tufted leather bench. She had on the one top hat he owned and had been pretending she was Fred Astaire a few moments earlier. Merri had loved all the Ginger Rogers and Fred Astaire movies, so Nolan had made sure that Daisey watched them.

"Just making sure I look okay. What do you think?" he asked as he turned to face her.

She hopped down from the bench and walked around him, and he felt her little hand on the hem of his jacket, straightening it slightly. "Good. Will you see Delaney tonight?"

"I don't know, Pip. She's got her own life, and she's very busy," he reminded her.

"I know," she said, sounding a little pouty.

He stooped so they were eye level. "She's got a lot of responsibilities. It might seem to you like she's just having fun, but her job is to make sure that celebrities and businesspeople like myself look good and are in the right place. She works just as hard as I do."

Something that had surprised him, but he knew that was because he'd expected her to be the Dish Soap Heiress that he'd read about on Wend-Z City. She was so much *more*. He wondered if she'd been waiting for him to get in touch with her.

He hadn't because sleeping with Delaney hadn't assuaged his lust for her. He still wanted her. Still hadn't figured out what made her tick. Still couldn't stop thinking about her—

"Okay, Daddy."

"Don't sound sad about it. You have your sleepover tonight with Thom, remember?"

"Yeah." She put the top hat back in its box and then skipped over to him. "You're right. We are going to be trying to find either a centaur or a unicorn. Even though they aren't real like fairies, Thom really likes them."

She shook her head. His daughter sounded the tiniest bit like him when she said that. The way he did when he was talking about his competitors, and it cracked him up, but also reminded him that he needed to be more careful with the way he compared himself to others to give himself the edge.

"Maybe you'll find one."

"I doubt it. I mean, they are both horse sized and Perri told Thom he couldn't have anything larger than one of those big yellow dogs."

"Golden retriever," he said.

"Yeah." He followed her down the hall to her bedroom where she had her overnight suitcase packed with her cloth doll sitting on top.

"Ready to go?"

"Yes," she said.

He dropped her off at Perri's house and then drove downtown toward the art museum where the event was being held. He valet parked his car and got out, heading toward the red carpet and the press who were waiting. He only got a few steps before Delaney appeared at his side.

She smelled like summer, and he almost reached out to pull her into his arms before stopping himself. She had on a gauzy yellow evening gown that made him forget about their plan for the evening, which was to raise Cooper Aeronautical's public profile and make him the face of it. And he *really* needed to be focused on dealing with the press, but he wasn't.

"Hey. Sorry to ambush you, but Malcolm arrived about ten minutes ago and I wanted to give you a heads-up on what he said so you can have your own message."

"Hi, Delaney." He met her eyes. "I didn't know you were attending."

"I wasn't planning to, but then I saw an alert that Malcolm was coming and I figured I should be here in case he said anything about the Mars mission."

"Did he?"

"Yes. He mentioned it…" She trailed off as she scrolled on her phone and then shook her head. "He said unlike his competitors he's focused on getting our people safely to Mars and not building play areas for children."

Dick.

"I'm not going to mention him. If anyone brings up the museum, I'll tell them how proud I am to help bring space to young minds and shape the future. What do you think?" he asked her, trying not to notice how the yellow gauzy material of her evening dress hugged her curves in all the right places and made her seem more ethereal than normal.

Delaney had made up her mind to keep her distance and be more professional where Nolan was concerned. It had been hard. Sometimes when she went to the Cooper Aeronautical building she'd catch a glimpse of him walking down the hall, and her dopamine levels would go all screwy and she'd find herself in a dreamy reverie of their hot night together…

Now, she couldn't help looking at his mouth and remembering it on her body. She had to clench her hands into fists to keep from touching him.

She also had to work really hard to keep herself from giving in to the feelings that seemed to be saying that Nolan was the man for her. Except he wasn't. He was

the means to an end. And a client. Not to mention a wid-
owed single dad. Frankly, the more she thought about
Nolan on paper the less it seemed like the two of them
should ever have hooked up.

And at the same time standing this close to him it
was all she could do to keep from throwing herself in
his arms and kissing him. As if the taste of him had
been imprinted on her brain and now she was starv-
ing for him.

Which she wasn't going to let happen. She had decided to channel all of the DNA her father had passed
on to her and be focused on her business goals. For once
in her life she was trying to be more like her workaholic father.

"I think your plan sounds perfect," she told Nolan.
"I'll go ahead and make sure they know who you are
and give them the digital press kit we put together."

He shot her a surprised look. "You don't want to
walk with me?"

"You don't want me to. We want them focused on
you and not distracted by me and my connection to
Malcolm," she said.

"What better distraction than you on my arm?" he
said huskily. "We can ignore it and let them speculate."

She tipped her head to the side. "Did you sleep with
me to get at Malcolm?"

It hadn't occurred to her before that he might have
his own *get Quell Aerospace plan* that might involve
using her. She didn't begrudge him that if he did, but
she hadn't thought of it.

"No. I'm not that kind of man. I slept with you because I wanted *you*. Did you do it to get back at Malcolm?" he asked. Though he seemed just as calm on the outside as he had earlier, she sensed some undefined emotion simmering under the surface.

"No. It just…well, happened."

He arched an eyebrow at her. "Does that happen to you a lot?"

"Not as often as you'd think. Something about you makes me…well, forget my plans," she said.

"What plans?"

Damn. He also made her want to reveal things that she knew she needed to keep to herself. She shrugged.

"No biggie. Just things like don't sleep with the client. That kind of thing," she said.

He threw his head back and laughed, and she couldn't help smiling at him. He was a big, intimidating man until he laughed. Then he seemed so much more approachable.

"That's actually a *good* plan."

"I know. That's why I've been keeping my distance," she admitted.

"That's the reason? I thought maybe you were waiting for me to make another move," he said.

"Were you going to make one?"

"I don't know," he replied. "You're not what I expected, Delaney, and I keep going around in my head about what is smart and what is…well, irrational. We are very different people, and though our circles sometimes cross we don't move in the same ones."

He wasn't saying anything she hadn't told herself more than once. But whereas for her that made her want to spend more time with him, she had the feeling for Nolan that just reinforced the fact that he should keep her at arm's length.

"Are mine worse than yours?" she asked. She knew she shouldn't have asked, but she needed to know. Something about Nolan made her want him to have some respect for her, maybe not all of her decisions or her methods, but she…wanted him not to see her as the hot mess that her father always did.

"Not at all. I'd say better. So are you walking in on my arm or not?" he asked.

"I guess so. Then I think we just go in and not say anything. You are giving a speech later. We can let that be the headline," she said. There was more than one way to make a statement, and sometimes silence spoke volumes. Also given that Nolan didn't really like making a tit-for-tat comment to everything Malcolm said, this might be a better approach.

"Perfect. You know I would prefer to never speak to the press."

"I do. But we should stop and pose for a picture. Both smiling at the camera. Like we're here together but are we *together* kind of pose," she said. "You'll get a lot of mileage out of it. That's what I did last week for Bryan Todd. His ex has really been making things rough for him and his image."

"So that's what you were doing with him? I wondered if it was work or just your life."

"My life and my work often dovetail together. I do attend a lot of these events because I'm on the board or the Alexander Corporation is and they might ask me to represent them. I rarely go for fun," she said.

"What *do* you do for fun?" he asked as they got closer to the press and their turn on the red carpet.

"Hunt fairies," she said with a wink as they were announced and walked into the sea of flashbulbs and yelled questions. They paused and smiled at the photographers and Nolan said nothing, but after a moment, he put his hand on the small of her back, directing her into the building.

Delaney felt the heat of his touch through her clothing and all the way to her core. And in that moment, she knew that she hadn't really put him into a client category after all. She still wanted more than one night with him, and that still wasn't wise.

Eleven

The charity event had been a lot of fun, but Nolan had made himself say goodbye to Delaney and leave early. And he was glad he did when he got to the office the next morning and got an email from his government contact informing him that the bidding office was launching an official investigation into Quell Aerospace.

Satisfied that the information was in the right hands, he knew that he should put it out of his mind, but he couldn't help but remember how many times Delaney had "shown" up with information right after Malcolm Quell did. It wasn't that he didn't trust her—it was that he was *afraid* to trust her.

That said, he had no evidence that she was up to anything with Quell. And perhaps his reluctance really stemmed from his attraction to her. Because no matter that he was high-fiving himself for leaving early and not kissing her as he'd longed to do all evening, he knew that he'd spent the entire night reliving their hookup and regretting not bringing her back to his place.

Everything about Delaney at work was tied to his fears of her in his personal life. Part of it was easily explainable even to himself. He didn't want to see Daisey hurt. But he knew there was more to it than that. He didn't want to get hurt again, either.

He'd loved one woman in his thirty-three years, and when she'd died six years ago, he'd shut that part of himself down.

"Heya, boss. Saw you all over the Wend-Z City site this morning. Looked as if you and Delaney were having fun."

Perri leaned on the door frame, smiling over at him. She'd set him up several times with women from her circle, but none of them had left a lasting impression the way Delaney did.

"It was business, Perri."

She raised her eyebrows at him. "What kind of business has you two looking like you can't keep your hands off each other?"

"The word-of-mouth, gossip business apparently," he said. "Our resident expert assured me it would work, and no one would be talking about anything Quell said."

"Well, she got that right," Perri mused. "Even the radio shows this morning were talking about you two, not a peep about Quell."

"Who was right?" Delaney asked, coming around the corner.

She gave him a smile as she handed Perri an iced latte. And then she perched on the edge of his desk, handing him a tall Americano.

"You," he said. "Thanks for this."

"Seemed rude to just get myself a drink," she told him. "And I like being right."

"I know," he said again.

"I don't know if it was all just a cover. Seems like you two get on pretty well," Perri said.

"We do," Delaney agreed. "Oh, and FYI…we are going to need to use the conference room to go through the prep for Nolan's appearance at the press conference later today. Can you help Hal set it up, Perri?"

"I can. I'll leave you two alone," she said, wriggling her eyebrows at them as she closed the door behind her.

"Sorry, she's a little bit—"

"Fabulous. Actually, she's a lot *fabulous* if I'm being honest. Everyone else around here is scared to say what's on their mind in case they offend you," Delaney said.

"Not everyone."

"Who else?"

His lips quirked. "You."

"Me again? Well, the truth is I'm intimidated by everyone so I have to just shove it down and be blunt," Delaney murmured, taking a sip of her coffee.

"I don't believe that for a second," he said.

This was precisely why he was struggling to trust her. She was fun in a way that Merri hadn't been. She was different from his type. In fact, he was pretty sure that Delaney didn't fall into any specific category. There was just *her*.

He glanced at his laptop screen and noticed that the email from the government official was still open and frowned as he clicked to close it.

"Is everything okay?" Delaney asked.

"Yeah, of course," he said.

"You looked a little bit concerned. Did Malcolm do something that hasn't shown up on my alert?"

"It's nothing. Just a question I forwarded to one of my government contacts. They are starting an investigation and I hope that they get results," he told her. That was as much as he was comfortable sharing right now.

She nodded, took another sip of her drink, and then opened her large purse and pulled out a present adorned in pink ribbons and wrapped in some kind of sparkly paper.

"You shouldn't have," he said when she handed it to him.

"Dang it! I only got one for Daisey, I'll have to owe you," she replied with a wink. "I hope you don't mind, but I saw this and knew she had to have it."

"What is it?"

"Just a small painting by an artist I know. It's called *Fairies at Play*," she said.

"Did you go to Pamela's gallery to get it?" he asked.

"Yes. I did. How'd you know?"

"Because I've been eyeing this piece for the last few months," he admitted. He hadn't gone back because he had been annoyed with Pamela after the wedding.

"I can't let you give Daisey a gift like this," he said. "It's too much."

She started laughing. "I think you're the first person to say that to me. Everyone expects the expensive gifts from me. I'm the dish soap heiress, Nolan."

"You're so much more than that," he said.

"That's a first too." She smiled softly. "Well, almost first. My besties know I'm more than what the public sees. Thank you for seeing the real me."

If only he could admit that he did. He had noticed that he'd hurt her by rejecting the painting and had sought to make amends, but now he wondered if he'd gone too far. She was more than the scandalous heiress, but that didn't make it easier to trust her or to trust himself around her.

Delaney tried not to let his words make her heart beat a little bit faster, but the truth was she wanted to just let go. Let her usual impulsiveness free and just fall hard for Nolan. But she wasn't going to.

Really.

Except when he leaned back in his chair, she couldn't help but stare at his strong square jawline and remember the way it had felt when she'd held his face in her hands and kissed him. She couldn't really concentrate on anything but his mouth then. Those firm lips that had been pursed and looked stern a few moments ago had felt so perfect against hers.

"You're staring at me," he said faintly.

"I can't help myself sometimes," she said, then blew him a kiss and hopped off his desk. "I better go and make sure everything's all set for your presentation. We need you in the conference room in five."

"Remind me again why Hal can't do this?"

Delaney shook her head. She had to admit she didn't get his reluctance to be in the spotlight. She'd sort of always craved it. Even when she had to take a back seat to a client, she was always a little bit envious.

"You're the name and the face of the company, not Hal. When you say it, you give it an authenticity that consumers and the public are going to associate with you. Does that make sense? Like even though a big corporation owns Disney, everyone still gets all warm and fuzzy thinking about Walt and being a part of his dream."

He shook his head. "I'm not going to do a weekly television show no matter how nicely you ask."

"Don't say no until you've heard my pitch," she said with a wink and then turned to leave before she made him an offer that was definitely more naughty than nice.

Perri was back at her desk and on the phone when Delaney walked by, but she stopped her with a hand on her wrist and mouthed the words *thank you* while pointing to her iced latte.

She just nodded and continued down the hall. Unlike Quell Aerospace, which had an old-world slash old money vibe to it, here at Cooper Aeronautical the art on the walls were designs of their successful space vehicles and the habitation pod that had been green-lighted by the government. She liked to think that Nolan was more concerned about what he was doing now than on looking back.

A bit like the man himself.

Also it helped her feel a little better about not sharing too many other details that she'd seen in Malcolm's mansion. Nolan wasn't a man to look for a leg up or dwell on the past…two things that should have reassured her, but it only worried her.

Because for the first time in a relationship, she wasn't rushing in and letting her soft heart rule her decisions. At times she felt like she was out of control and not sure what to do next. Other times, like last night at the museum, she'd just followed her business instincts and it had paid off. But that was brand and image. She was the queen at mastering those.

The painting for Daisey…that felt a bit like it hadn't been. She knew that Nolan didn't want her to be friends with his daughter because Daisey had texted her and told her not to mention it to her dad.

She still wasn't sure if she would or not. She wasn't about to pursue a friendship with a six-year-old, but at the same time, there was something about the sweet, bubbly little girl that made her laugh. And seeing her and Nolan together…well, it was just what her wounded inner child needed to see.

"Hey, Delaney. I hope these boards will do. I had the art department work on them overnight. We can make some tweaks if needed and print off new ones before his press conference later."

Hal was a fun guy to work with and from what Delaney could tell really loved his job. He was her age and had curly hair, a neatly trimmed beard and warm hazel eyes. The man worked long hard hours but always had time for anything she asked him for, and he always had a quip and a smile.

Why couldn't she fall for someone like Hal? He would be perfect for a fling or whatever. He was nice and easy. Not like tall, dark and broody back there.

"I'm sure they're great," she told him. "Also, um, how do you feel about pranking your boss?"

"Not good. I need this job. But what did you have in mind?" he asked.

"Just wanted you to teasingly bring up doing a thirty-minute television show sort of like Walt Disney did when he was opening the Orlando theme park."

"Are you trying to get one of my loyal employees in the scheme I already said no to?" Nolan asked.

Delaney turned to find Nolan standing behind her, both eyebrows lifted as if he were teasing her. She shook her head and turned back to Hal.

Hal just smiled at her. "Busted. Sorry, Delaney, he walked in just as you said it."

"That's okay, I just like to start meetings with some fun. Don't mind if I'm the one getting pranked."

Hal laughed and turned to finish adjusting the boards. "So you like pranks?"

"Um, sometimes. I mean, I like stuff like this that is clearly good fun and teasing. I don't like to see anyone get hurt emotionally or physically, though."

Nolan hadn't intended on spending the entire day with Delaney. But somehow his prep session had turned into project brainstorming and a working lunch, and then she went with him to the press conference, which had stretched into the dinner hour and…he wanted to take her out.

He'd texted Daisey already and talked to her nanny, so he wasn't needed at home.

"Want to grab dinner?" he asked when they'd finished the press conference. He didn't want the day with her to end, and she was the only person other than Daisey he felt that way about lately. And while he still didn't fully trust her, he was tired of fighting himself where she was concerned. He wanted to at least give himself a chance to see if there was more here. And taking her out to dinner was the perfect way to find out.

"Another working meal? I think we've covered it all," she said.

"I was thinking more a date than work," he said gruffly. "Is that crossing a line?"

"Not at all. I'd love to have dinner with you. But I have to let Stanley out and take him for a walk first. My dog walker is on vacation this week…and it's fajita and margaritas night with my friends and their boyfriends. Want to come or would it be awkward?"

He hesitated. Meet her friends… He had asked her on a date so what was the difference? But in his mind there was one.

"Were you hoping for a quick shag?"

When she put it that way he felt like an ass. "No, that's not it. I just don't know your friends, and I'm not always the best in social situations."

She started laughing. "You'll like them, I promise. You already know Olive and Paisley are my business partners so you might know a bit about them from our prospectus. And Olive is engaged to Dante Russo so he'll be there and Paisley has been living with Jack... I literally don't know his last name."

"Okay," he said. She kind of relaxed when she talked about her friends, and it was like he was seeing yet another side of her. "Why don't you know his last name?"

"I don't think that Paisley's ever said it, but if she did it would be rude for me to ask again. And she's super protective of her privacy so unless she brings him up I don't." Delaney shrugged. "But he's a lot of fun."

"Where is this fajitas and margaritas gathering happening?"

She told him the name of the restaurant and bar where she and her friends met once a week. He nodded. "I'll meet you there. I should go back to the office and change."

"Okay or you could come to my place, and we could go over together. I don't live too far from there."

He was curious about where she lived. Would he learn more about her if he saw it? "Sounds great. But I still need to change. I can't go out like this."

"What were you planning to wear on our date?"

"This. I was going to suggest the club again," he said. "Business suits were the norm there."

She texted him her address. "Get ready and meet me. This is going to be so much fun. Normally I'm the fifth wheel, but this week I won't be."

"You're the fifth wheel?" he asked, not entirely sure that someone as social as Delaney could ever be called that.

"Don't get me started. It used to be girls' night, and

then Paisley met Jack and started bringing him, then Olive got engaged and now I have you."

"Uh."

"Calm down, Nolan. I have you for *tonight*. Does that make your butt cheeks unclench?"

He shook his head, putting his hand on the small of her back and directing her out of the building to the waiting cars. "They weren't clenched."

"You looked like you'd just been caught with the wrong person by the paparazzi," she said.

"Well, you're a sexy, beautiful woman, but I haven't thought about long-term," he admitted. "Have you?"

"Not really. You have a kid, and you don't want us to be friends and it's complicated," she said, waving her hand. A moment later, a silver Rolls pulled up.

"Is this your car?"

"Yes. I lost my driver's license years ago and now I have Lyle."

"Why?"

"Driving under the influence too many times, and I crashed my car on Michigan Avenue. Ring any bells?" she asked. "Also, I like it better now. Driving always made me so nervous."

It did ring bells, but this Delaney bore little resemblance to that woman. It was almost ten years ago that she'd done that. He remembered the photos and the headlines. She'd come a long way from that woman.

"I just don't associate you with that incident. What did you mean about you and Daisey being friends?" he asked, gesturing to her driver to stay in the car as he opened the door for Delaney.

"Well, don't rat me out, but she texted me some info on fairies she thought I'd be interested in but told me not to mention it to you."

That little sneak. How had she even gotten Delaney's number? "I just don't know that you're the ideal friend for a six-year-old."

"I totally agree. I thanked her for the info and said it would be better to text me with you next time. She hasn't texted since."

He met her eyes and murmured in a gentler tone, "She really likes you, Delaney."

"I like her too, but as I said, it's complicated. And I remember being a little girl and hoping each woman my dad dated would be my new mom," she told him.

"Thank you." Really, it was all he could say to her. She'd thought of his daughter and done what was best for her.

That type of altruism wasn't what he associated with Delaney, and it made him rethink everything he knew about her. She got into her car and he watched her drive away, but his mind was on the fact that she'd done what was best for his daughter and not herself.

She hadn't taken advantage of the opening she'd been given into his private life. Which meant she had more moral strength than he'd given her credit for. He had to admit the more he got to know her, the less sure he was of any of the impressions he'd had of her.

Twelve

Inviting Nolan to margaritas and fajitas had been a calculated risk. Her friends knew that she was working with him, but Delaney had kept the fact that they'd hooked up to herself. They *did* know that she'd started out getting to know him because he was a competitor of Malcolm's so...she hadn't wanted to seem even more ditzy than normal by telling them that she was starting to fall for Nolan.

But when she sent a message in their group text that she was bringing a date, both Paisley and Olive had texted back. Finally, we can't wait to meet Nolan.

Delaney: Uh, how?

Olive: You are spending way too much time with him. He's your favorite client.

Paisley: Plus, we saw the photos online this morning. He might have fallen for the "this will distract the press" line, but you like him.

It was true. She had been trying to tell herself that no one else could see it but her friends had.

Delaney: Was it obvious?

Olive: Just to us. Even Dante didn't pick up on it.

Paisley: Yeah, don't sweat it.

Delaney: Good. See you later.

She loved the way that Olive made it seem like Dante would have noticed if she'd been overt about her interest in Nolan. As much as her friend had changed from a former bad girl who spent most of her time manipulating people into doing things for her, she still didn't always see people for who they were. And Dante was a dude and not really tuned into what women were feeling, other than Olive.

When she got home, she let Stanley out, fed and cuddled him, then changed into a halter neck jumpsuit. It was vintage Halston and had been her mom's. It was in a crisp gold color that had been the rage in the '70s. She paired it with wedge heels and a chunky resin bracelet. Afterward, she pulled her hair into a high ponytail and did her makeup in a more natural way but couldn't resist a sexy red lip.

As she clocked herself in the mirror, she realized that it was a good thing Olive and Paisley had already figured out she was into Nolan because this outfit was a little extra for girls' night. Not that she minded.

She blew herself a kiss in the mirror and headed down to her living room to wait for Nolan. But she didn't have to wait long. The doorbell rang just as she'd poured herself a seltzer water.

Stanley barked excitedly and followed her down the hall to the door. She opened it and stepped back, taking in Nolan. He wore a pair of dark wash jeans and a patterned button-down shirt that showed his broad shoulders to advantage. His dark hair was neat, and she could tell he'd shaved his five o'clock shadow.

She noticed he was checking her out too. When he finished, he let out a wolf whistle.

"Wow. You look amazing," he said.

"You too. This is Stanley, and he'll pretty much keep wagging his entire body until you say hi," she said. Then had a horrible thought. "Unless you don't like dogs?"

"Love 'em," he said, squatting and petting Stanley. And he even let the French bulldog lick his face.

Once Stanley had greeted him, he turned and trotted back to his bed. Nolan stood up, wriggling his eyebrows at her. "Want a kiss? I need to get the taste of Stanley out of my mouth."

She shook her head and pointed him to the powder room. "There's mouthwash in the medicine cabinet."

"I was kidding. I didn't let the dog lick inside my mouth," he said. "You ready to go?"

"Let me grab my bag and set the alarm. Lyle is standing by. He'll take you home too, if you want, so you can drink and have fun."

"That's nice. But I took an Uber over and can take one home later," he said.

"Whatever you decide." She set the alarm after she texted Lyle, and then they were ready to go.

When they got in the back of the Rolls, she realized that Nolan hadn't been difficult about any part of this night. Malcolm hadn't gone to meet her friends when they'd dated because he said that eating in a chain restaurant and bar was too plebian. As if he were royalty or something. At the time she had told herself that he just had discerning taste, but in retrospect she realized that he'd never really wanted to know the people in her life except for her father's business acquaintances.

"I love that outfit," he said.

"Thank you again. It was my mom's, and my dad's assistant had all her clothes put in storage for me until I was older. It was such a nice present when I turned eighteen."

"That is a nice idea. I kept a few of Merri's things for Daisey, and I try to keep her alive by sharing things she loved."

"Like what?"

"Movies from the '30s and '40s, Trixie Belden mysteries and buttered pecan ice cream," he said.

"I love it. I've never read the Trixie Belden books. Are they good?"

"Yeah, they are a bit like Nancy Drew and the Hardy Boys. Daisey and Thom spent most of the summer trying to solve mysteries around the house. Our house-keeper was interrogated more than once to make sure she hadn't seen anyone stealing cookies."

Delaney had to laugh at that. Nolan had clearly done a lot to keep Daisey's mom in her life, something her father hadn't been able to do. After the Michigan Avenue driving incident, he'd mentioned her mother for the first time, only to say that she would have been disappointed in the woman that Delaney had become.

They'd had an ugly fight after that, but his words had resonated with her and been a wake-up call she hadn't realized she'd needed.

"I have been trying for the last few years to be a woman my mom would be proud of," she said out loud.

"I can't imagine she wouldn't be," Nolan murmured, then leaned over to kiss her.

Delaney kissed him back and realized she was almost allowing herself to believe that she could make this work with him. Almost.

It was hard not to feel welcomed by the group. Olive and Dante had been waiting at a tall table near the back of the restaurant and waved them over as soon as they arrived. Olive and Delaney immediately left for the bathroom.

"I'm Dante, by the way. Olive is my fiancée," he said. "The ladies tend to get all into their conversations so figured I'd introduce myself first."

"Nolan," he said, offering the other man his hand. "Nothing official with Delaney."

As soon as he said it, he felt a bit icky inside. There

was a connection between the two of them, and he could have just acknowledged it. But he wasn't Delaney. He didn't live his life for the rest of the world. If there was something to say about them as a couple, he'd say it to her first.

"It's cool. So this place is more bar than restaurant. Usually the girls talk and don't eat much. Jack and I decided to add fajitas to their usual margaritas, and it's been a hit. But we're going to have to go to the bar to order food and drinks."

"Thanks. So...what do you do?" he asked. It was his standard ice-breaking question. But also, he felt like he recognized the other guy's voice. He felt like he knew him, but had never met him before.

"Uh, I make beer," he said.

Dante... Inferno Brewing. "Duh. I thought you sounded familiar. I'm a big fan of the 9th Circle."

"Thanks."

"How'd you and Olive meet?" he asked because he had no beer conversation to make. He knew sweet FA about brewing.

"Truth?"

He nodded.

"In college I was a tubby frat boy nerd and asked her out and she shot me down, then my company hired her to help with my brand launch. I was sort of slimmed down but more of a mountain man than this," he said, gesturing to himself. "Olive helped make me over and get me ready for being the public face of Inferno Brewing."

"What are you two talking about?" Olive asked as

she and Delaney returned and she hopped up onto the stool next to Dante.

"Just filling Nolan in on how we met."

"That's right, you two met the same way," Olive said, gesturing to himself and Delaney.

"Uh, I wasn't a tubby—"

"*Dante Russo!* Did you tell him about the first time we met?" Olive asked, turning to face her fiancé.

"Yeah. It's the truth. I'm not going to pretend it didn't happen, and you shouldn't, either," he said gently to her.

"I hate that person I was."

"Well, I love her because she made you who you are today," he said, pulling her into his arms and Nolan assumed he was kissing her, but he turned to face Delaney.

"So we order at the bar?"

"Yeah, let's go get a round of drinks while those two do what they do," she said, linking her arm through his.

"Did she really turn him down?" he asked.

"Yeah. He had taken the deejay's microphone and made this big ole speech and Olive…well, back then she was the queen b, and her rejection was pretty cutting."

"How did they get together after all that?" Nolan asked. "I mean, if it's okay to ask…"

"It's fine," she told him. "Olive changed a lot. A girl in our sorority reported her for bullying, and she had to go to therapy and do community service—we did it together—and it really changed her. She's worked hard to distance herself from the woman she was back then. Dante loves all versions of Olive, though, so he won't let her just ignore that part of herself. He says, well, I guess you heard him."

Nolan was impressed by the work that Olive had done. He knew he could be a demanding boss, but he always tried to make sure he didn't cross into overbearing, which wasn't always easy when he wanted things done. "She's come a long way."

"Yeah, she has. We all have. Do you remember being twenty and an 'adult'?"

He laughed when she made air quotes, then felt a punch in his gut as he realized how much he liked her. He might have been able to pretend to himself earlier that he was just testing things out with her, but a part of him already felt possessive of her and that she was already his. "Yeah, I do. I was so sure that I knew everything."

"*Did* you? You sort of strike me as one of those people who has always had himself together," she said.

"Not really. I have always been big and clean-cut, so everyone kind of looks to me to lead in situations. So I had to mature pretty quick."

She turned and hugged him, cupping his butt as she did so. "I can see that. You do have a natural leadership vibe about you."

He put his hands on her waist and lifted her up, kissing her quick and deep because he wanted to. "Thanks."

He set her on her feet and she hooked her arm through his so that he felt the brush of her side boob against his arm.

"Paisley says some of us take longer to grow up," Delaney said. "I definitely am more that type. At first, I was just, like, I'm out from under my old man's thumb, so why not party all the time, but then after the Michigan Avenue crash and community service, I realized I wasn't at all adult and needed to figure out what would make me feel like one."

"Have you?" he asked after he ordered their drinks and food.

She shook her head and gave him a wry grin. "Not really. I mean, I'm not the hot mess express I used to be, but most days I'm still kind of surprised by how together I am. You?"

"I have Daisey so I feel like I should say yes, but the truth is I'm winging it like you."

"Like *everyone* I suspect," she said.

The bartender gave them a tray with margaritas and a coaster for their table that would alert the waiter for their food. Nolan reached for his wallet, but Delaney had her card out and gave it to the bartender.

"Put everything on here and open a tab," she said.

When the bartender turned away, he looked down at her and she arched both eyebrows at him. "Are you going to argue with me paying? It's the twenty-first century."

"I was going to say thank you."

She eyed him as if trying to decide if she should believe him or not but then just nodded.

She was a very generous woman, and it wasn't just with her money but with her smiles and general kindness. He tried to tell himself that didn't make him fall a little bit for her, but he was tired of pretending he didn't like her. A lot.

* * *

Delaney didn't allow herself to worry or think about anything but her friends and Nolan. He'd turned her on with that kiss at the bar and had kept his hand on her back for most of the night. She felt a kind of euphoria, which was unusual since normally when she was out, she was thinking about the paparazzi and what they might capture. But the truth was, she felt almost free tonight, laughing and talking with her friends.

All of them had someone now, and for the first time in months, Delaney didn't feel like the fifth wheel.

"Jack, you're looking mighty tan," Delaney said when she had a moment to talk to Paisley's man. He had thick brown hair, dark brown eyes and the kind of smile that the camera loved.

"Yeah, had to take my gran to Florida to see her friends in the Shady Beaches Retirement Community."

"Did you drive?" she asked. "I mean, I think Paisley said that."

"Yeah. Gran doesn't like to fly."

"I don't blame her. Flying commercial is an affront to personal happiness," she said. "You're welcome to use my private jet the next time she wants to visit her friends."

She suspected that Jack and his gran were pinching pennies based on a few things that Paisley had let slip about him. He used her Netflix and Apple accounts. And almost always suggested they eat in at her place— where he lived rent free instead of going out—which to Delaney just seemed to indicate he didn't have a lot of money.

"Thanks. She'd love that," he said.

"No problem. I'd love to meet her. I bet Gran would liven up a party."

Jack looked a bit uncomfortable, and Delaney realized she might have overstepped. He and Paisley had been living together for almost six months, but he might not be ready for her to meet his gran or for her to interact with Paisley's friends.

"I never knew my grandmothers. But I did have a great-aunt who was a bit like Auntie Mame. She'd walk into a room, all furs and satin with a long cigarette and saying outrageous things."

He laughed. "Sounds like an interesting character."

"She was. She'd been cut out of the dish soap inheritance because she'd run off with the love of her life. He was penniless and not from the right sort of family—back when that sort of thing mattered. Anyway, he died in Vietnam and Auntie Gray has mourned him ever since. So tragic."

"What's tragic?" Nolan asked, turning to join their conversation.

"Losing love," Jack replied.

"Yes, it is," he said. "Have you?"

Jack looked pensively at Paisley and then shook his head. Delaney wondered why he'd looked at her friend.

"You?" he asked Nolan.

Oh, no.

"Yes, my wife. Delaney?"

"I've lost too many loves to count," she said, trying to lighten the mood by steering the conversation back to her scandalous past. She knew Nolan didn't want to discuss his deceased wife.

"Too many loves or lovers?" Nolan asked.

"Is there a difference? My auntie Gray said a woman should fall in love often," Delaney murmured.

"After she lost her true love?" Jack asked.

"Yes. She said that true love only comes once in a lifetime, but there are other types of love."

"Interesting," Nolan said.

"Yeah. She was a character, that's for sure. Did you try the shrimp fajitas? They are really good with the mango salsa and black beans," she said, pointing to the food. Desperate to get off this subject. What had she been thinking?

Then she remembered it had been her who'd diverted the topic when she'd tried to get to meet Jack's gran. Nolan made her a fajita, and they talked about Mexico and their trips there. But she knew that something had changed for Nolan. She didn't have to be that girl detective he'd mentioned to figure out that bringing up his dead wife had put a damper on the evening for him.

He was human…that was to be expected. But she had wanted this night to go well for them. A chance to be a real couple without worrying about Malcolm or Cooper Aeronautical or him being Daisey's dad.

She felt selfish even thinking those things, and considering the man that Nolan was, she knew that he was always carrying Daisey's mom with him. He wasn't anything like her father had been, and she knew that was part of why she liked him as much as she did.

But that difference was also making it harder for

her. She had no idea how to deal with him when he was being all real.

"You're not eating," Nolan remarked when Jack and Paisley went to get another round of drinks.

"I'm sorry the true love thing came up," she said.

He lifted a broad shoulder. "I'm not. It's not like she didn't exist."

"Of course, but that doesn't mean you want to talk about it with people you've just met."

"True. When you and I talk about her, it doesn't feel intrusive," he admitted. "How did you two start talking about true love anyway?"

She felt all warm and fuzzy inside at the thought of not being intrusive. "I was trying to find out more about his grandma and he shut it down, so then I started down a path that led to my auntie Gray."

"Of course you did," he said. "Why did you change the subject?"

"Because I felt like I'd overstepped."

"Something you tend not to concern yourself about," he mused.

"I know, but Paisley really likes him, and I don't want to do anything to hurt that," she said.

"Why would you?"

She shrugged. How could she tell this man who still held his deceased wife in high regard that most people didn't hold her in the same esteem? She was impulsive and said things that often led to awkward situations, and Paisley and Olive were the sisters she'd never had. She would never do anything to hurt them or the people they loved, and there had been a moment when she'd felt like she might have with Jack.

"I'm not sure. Something I said seemed to make his walls come up, and I was backpedaling, hoping to undo it."

"I'm sure you imagined that. When have you not been the most enchanting woman in the room?" he asked with his most charming smile. He hugged her to his side.

She had to smile back. He was trying to cheer her up, and it was working.

Thirteen

Nolan got the urgent email forwarded to him from the government office informing him they'd finished their investigation and were inviting him to attend the congressional subcommittee meeting the following week, where they would be publishing the results. That was all the information contained in the message.

He looked at his calendar and saw that Perri had marked that Daisey had the week off from school for her fall break. And he'd already given the nanny the week off. She'd been sick and had asked to go home for two weeks. Which normally wasn't a problem because between himself and the housekeeper, they could handle Daisey when school was in session. But he knew his daughter would be upset if he was gone during her break. Normally, he'd bring her and the nanny with him. He had a brownstone in Georgetown that he kept for occasions like this.

He was running through the possibilities... Perri and her family were not an option since they'd booked a vacation to Cancun. And he doubted that she'd change her plans to come to DC. And his housekeeper couldn't travel.

"Hey, do you have time to discuss some notes for your press conference this afternoon?" Delaney asked, poking her head into his office. "Perri's not at her desk. Sorry for just popping in."

Her blond hair was pulled off to one side, and she wore a long flowing dress that ended at her calves with a pair of ridiculously high heels that were covered in a floral print and had rhinestones across the strap. It was all he could do to keep from getting up, locking his office door and taking her on his desk.

"It's fine," he said, gesturing for her to come inside and close the door behind her.

She did, sitting on the edge of his desk as was her habit. "So, I'm thinking it's time to up the wow factor in your press briefings. I like the down-to-earth rep you are getting, but now we need to follow it up with substance. I mean, we want them to see you as a Richard Branson sort, putting your money where your mouth is, but also showing progress."

"I'm not really much like Branson, but so far you haven't steered me wrong," he said, realizing how true that was.

Since that night six weeks ago when they'd gone to dinner with her friends, they'd spent more time together.

Some of it with Daisey, but most of it just the two of them. He wasn't sure if he was starting to like doing press or if he just liked it because he got to spend more time with Delaney while doing it. He'd wanted her back in his house, but other than a few hurried hookups in his office or at her place, they hadn't.

"I know. I'm the real deal when it comes to dealing with the press," she said with a cocky smile and a wink. "That was way easier than I expected. I still have four hours before my next meeting."

"Actually, I need your help on another project," he told her. Then he caught her up on the meeting in DC next week where an announcement would be made. He didn't go into the details, just saying he might need her to help him to quickly come up with a response to the situation.

"It would be better if I was with you in DC," she said. "Is that what you are asking?"

"Sort of. I want to bring Daisey too so we can have a little vacation in between the meetings." He suddenly realized that he wanted her there with him not as his brand manager but as his girlfriend. That stopped him in his tracks. But he'd already invited her and used the word *vacation* so there could be no turning back from it. And honestly? He didn't want to turn back. As much as he was wary of letting himself admit it, he cared for Delaney.

He knew that Daisey did too, and if this was going to ever become more than a sort of casual affair, he was going to have to start trusting again. Both himself and her. He admitted it was harder to trust himself than

Delaney. Everything he'd seen of her had shown him that he could believe in her.

"What are you asking me? I don't want to jump to the wrong conclusion," she said.

"That I want you to come with me and Daisey on a trip to DC and that we'd both have to do some work while we are there, but the job isn't the reason why I want you there."

Delaney squealed and jumped off his desk, running around to throw herself in his lap. She wrapped her arms around his shoulders, bringing her mouth down on his. Her hands framed his face and she tilted her head to the side, prompting him to deepen the kiss. Holding her head with his hand, he thrust his tongue into her mouth. He wanted her. It was starting to become a habit, and he didn't want to fight it. Then she lifted her head and their eyes met, and he saw so much in her eyes that it almost hurt him. There was a vulnerability to Delaney that her outer bad-girl, badass image belied, but he knew that it was there.

"I guess that's a yes."

"Of course it is. So I can be friends with Daisey now?" she asked. "You don't think I'm just an easy hookup?"

"Ah, yes to being friends and there is *nothing* easy about you, Delaney. As much as I wanted to pretend we could just do that and not have a relationship beyond it, I think we both know that's no longer true."

"I mean, you are still kind of my stud muffin client. Can I keep calling you that?" she asked.

He flushed at the name *stud muffin*. "Who do you call me that to?"

"Just Stanley and Olive and Paisley," she told him with a laugh.

"No, stop calling me that to your friends. It's okay to say it to Stanley, though," he said. "Will you need to bring him with us?"

"Unless it's a bother, I'd like to. We can take my jet. He's used to it," she said.

Her jet. He sometimes forgot about her fortune—not often because it was so much a part of her, yet at the same time, she was starting to become just Delaney and not the dish soap heiress.

Which suited him just fine.

Delaney knew she should probably temper her excitement, but Nolan had invited her to go away with him and Daisey, which was huge. *Huge!*

He'd limited their personal interactions to sex or late-night talks in his office, where he shared more memories of his wife and his childhood. Which had only served to make her fall even harder for him. But it had been the afternoon barbecue he'd invited her to help host for Daisey and a group of her school friends that had made her feel like he might be getting serious too.

She knew she had a history of filling in the blanks in relationships with the wrong emotions. Malcolm hadn't loved her, but she'd made him into the love of her life and he was simply the latest in a long line of men that she'd thought were the one.

Delaney tried to caution herself not to do the same

thing with Nolan, but this felt different. She was still perched on his lap when she heard the door to his office open. He turned and set her on her feet as Perri walked in with a stack of mail.

"Sorry, boss, didn't mean to interrupt. I thought you were alone," she said, hesitating in the doorway.

"Come on in. I was just going over the notes that Delaney had for me," he told his assistant. "Delaney and I are going to be in DC next week. I forwarded you an email and had asked you to schedule plane tickets for us and Daisey, but Delaney has offered us her jet. I do need you to still have the house in Georgetown opened and get us a housekeeper and driver for the week," he said.

She stood to the side watching him change into work mode. And wondered at how quickly he switched gears. Her body was still buzzing from his nearness, and she felt her heart beating too fast, but she knew she needed to dial it back. "Perri, can you forward me the details of the meeting so I can start working on some press—"

"I'll update you on the plane," he interjected. "The email doesn't really have any information in it."

"Okay," she said, but couldn't help thinking it was odd. But then government contracts could be and after the insider information that Malcolm had gotten, Nolan was probably determined to keep everything on a need-to-know basis. She respected his integrity and his morals.

"Is there anything else?" Perri asked.

"No, that's all for now. I'll be with Delaney for—how much longer do we need?" he asked her.

"An hour at most. I just want you to run through the

points that Hal and I have roughed out for you so it feels natural. Then I'll ask you some questions and see how you handle them," she said.

"Then maybe plan for two hours, Perri," he said.

"Will do. Can I order lunch for you both?"

He looked over at her and Delaney nodded. She was hungry and had a hankering for Italian.

"What do you want?"

"Portillo's. I know it's not healthy, but I haven't had Italian beef in so long, and I heard a commercial in the car on the way over," she admitted.

"Works for me," Nolan said. "Get yourself one too," he told his assistant. "Perri loves Portillo's."

"I do," she admitted. "I could eat from there every day."

Delaney smiled, and Perri left. Nolan looked over at her.

"Sorry for taking you off my lap. I just want to keep office protocols around the staff. Though we have a policy in place for those who want to date, it's not really encouraged, and I don't want to be seen as breaking our own rules," he said.

"Of course you don't."

He quirked one eyebrow at her. "Does it bother you?"

"Not really. One of the things I really like about you is the way you follow the rules."

That made him laugh and shake his head. "I made most of them, so it makes sense."

"I know. You like to set parameters, don't you?"

"And you like to break them."

"I do. Are you sure about me going with you and

Daisey?" she asked, as the more she thought about her past behavior, the less this seemed like the sure thing she wanted it to be.

"Yes and no. It's a risk. We both are very different people and see the world in our own way. Neither of us likes compromise, and there is a good chance this won't work out. But I'm not the kind of man who has regrets. And I have a feeling if I don't give this a chance..." He trailed off, not saying what they were both thinking.

"I'd regret it too," she admitted softly. "I guess we just both have to leap and hope the bridge will appear."

"Well, in real life I'd have on a parachute and maybe some crash pads but—"

"That's not a very romantic image, Nolan," she admonished. "Do you think you're going to need that stuff?"

Even as she spoke the words, she was no less sure of him now than she'd been earlier. Nolan had one thing in his favor that Malcolm never had, and that was that Nolan hadn't lied to her. He might not always say what she wanted to hear, but he never hedged. The man was straightforward, and she appreciated that more than he could ever know.

"I really don't know," he admitted. "The only thing I'm sure of is that I want you with me for more than hookups in my office and the odd weekend with Daisey. I care about you, Delaney, and as much as I'm scared to let myself go down the relationship path again, I can't stop it."

Nolan hadn't meant to get that personal, but there'd been no other choice. That said, he felt awkward opening himself up like that because he was unsure about where they stood, and that wasn't comfortable for him. With Merri he'd known they were building to a future and a family together. But with Delaney? Nothing was for sure. And she hadn't been kidding when she'd described the two of them. They were the complete opposite, and there were more moments than he wanted to admit when he wasn't sure that his feelings for her were real.

She was an enchantress not by guile but by instinct, and he couldn't resist her. But it wasn't just a male-female dynamic. Perri and Hal and Daisey and everyone Delaney met fell under her spell. She just charmed them all with her effervescent personality and genuinely kind heart.

"Wow, that was real. I think I owe you the truth too," she said.

His heart sort of dropped at her words. Had she not been honest with him? He didn't want to let his mind go there, but it did.

"What truth?"

"I care a lot about you too. I've been holding back because if you weren't willing to let me be in Daisey's life, I knew that we'd never have anything more than sex between us. And I wanted…well, so much more." She sighed. "I know I'm not the girl next door and I have my scandalous reputation, but honestly, I'm just a girl and my heart can break just like any other person's."

The way she spoke with such raw honesty got to him. He had a feeling that she'd had her heart broken more than once. The thing about Delaney was, she looked like she was up for anything and that she was skating through life on the surface. But more and more he was coming to realize that she felt things more deeply than anyone ever noticed.

Until him.

Or that was what he was telling himself. He might be falling for the biggest con ever, but his gut said he wasn't. It said it was safe to trust her not only in his bed but in his life and in his business.

"I see that," he said softly. "I mean, you are way too extravagant in your gift giving, but there is a realness to you beneath all of that."

"Thanks, Nolz, you know how to turn a girl's head."

He shook his. "I try."

Their eyes locked and held for a long, palpable moment, but finally, she released a breath and broke the silence. "I can't believe I'm saying this, but we need to get back to working on your points for the press conference. I don't want to slow down your momentum, and right now you're the *it* guy. Which of course will only last as long as you keep generating new and exciting content for the media to use."

He respected what she was saying and wanted her even more when she showed her business acumen. She was so many different women to him, and each one was just as attractive as the other. He might be intimidated by her wealthy socialite side, but he still respected it.

"Where are my notes?"

"Hal was supposed to email you," she said, coming to stand over his shoulder.

He started to open his emails but hesitated when he remembered that the one about the meeting next week, which specifically mentioned the concerns he'd raised about Quell Aerospace, was still in his inbox.

And he wasn't sure if he wanted her to see that. "Why don't you grab Hal and I'll meet you both in the conference room. I think he asked to have the teleprompters set up there."

She tipped her head to the side, studying him, and he was reminded of how she'd looked when they'd been playing chess. Which was totally not the analogy he wanted to make right now when he was trying to convince himself she wasn't playing a long game with him and Malcolm.

"Is there something you don't want me to see?" she asked.

He squared his shoulders and gave her a hard look. "A lot of my correspondence is sensitive information. I can't just open it while you're standing here."

She nodded. "Of course. Sorry, I didn't think of that. I shouldn't have stood so close. I'll be in the conference room."

She turned to walk away, but he stood and stopped her, catching her arm with his hand. When she turned, he saw the hurt in her eyes, but she herself had said that Malcolm had been loose with information. She had to realize there were consequences for that.

"Don't take it personally."

"It's hard for it not to feel that way," she said. "I know about confidentiality. You could have just asked me to step away. I hadn't realized what I was doing."

"What would you have said if I'd been blunt and asked you to move?"

"Moved. I'm not trying to pry into your business, Nolan. Even my business has a lot of information that can't be shared. Clients who are caught doing something that will ruin their careers and businesses. I should have thought of that."

"Why didn't you?" he asked.

"I was still just thinking about you asking me to go away with you," she admitted quietly. "I know, not very professional. I think I'm beginning to understand your HR policy on dating. It is distracting."

"Very," he agreed. "And it leads to hard feelings and sometimes leaked information."

She nodded. "Won't happen again. In fact, I shouldn't have hopped on your lap to begin with," she said.

"No, Delaney, you shouldn't have." He pulled her into his arms and brought his mouth down hard on hers, kissing her long and deeply like he'd wanted to since Perri had left the office. "I'm glad you did."

"Me too," she said breathlessly.

He stepped away from her and opened the door. Perri was standing at her desk with the Portillo's bags. "Lunch in the conference room?"

"Yes," he said. "Go on and I'll be there in a minute."

Delaney and Perri walked away, both women talking to each other, and he watched them until they were out of sight. He wanted to trust her as much as his body wanted her, but he had some new doubts stirring and he hoped this next week would lay them to rest.

Fourteen

The late summer heat held on in DC, but that didn't seem to bother either of the Coopers as they explored all of the tourist sites and took photos at each one. Delaney adored the way that Nolan was with Daisey, and it was getting harder and harder to pretend she wasn't falling in love with him.

She knew that there was much more to a relationship than what the last few months had shown her, but in her bones, this seemed real. More real than any family she'd ever had in her life, except for her sisterhood with Olive and Paisley.

She'd always been the dish soap heiress in her family. The lucky one who through the circumstances of her birth inherited every bit of a fortune that had through tradition and determination passed to the oldest grandchild. And that had always made her feel like an outsider in her own family.

"Delaney, let's try to push over the big thing over there," Daisey said, gesturing to the Washington Memorial. Yesterday they'd taken several photos where they used forced perspective to make it seem like they were touching different monuments around the city.

"Okay, let's do it! Where should we stand, Nolan?" she asked.

He looked through the lens of his camera and gave them directions, and a moment later, Delaney found herself standing over Daisey, acting as if the two of them were pushing the Memorial. Nolan took several shots. Daisey skipped back to him, and Delaney pulled her phone out of her purse to snap some photos of the father and daughter together as Nolan scooped up his little girl and put her on his shoulders.

"I hope you don't mind me saying, but you have a beautiful family," an older lady said as she and her husband paused. "Reminds me of so many happy times we had when our kids were young. You're a very lucky lady."

Delaney could only smile and nod. Except she hadn't ever felt lucky. Not really. She had crashed her car into a retail store in front of numerous paparazzi. Worst of all, she had set herself up to meet this man she was in love with for revenge.

The couple moved on and Nolan came over to her.

"What did they want?"

"Just to say how cute we were," she said. This weekend seemed to be a sort of tentative test for them as a couple, so she decided against mentioning the lady thought they were a family.

It just seemed safer.

Except when had she ever made the safer choice? As much as she felt comfortable being herself with Nolan, she also didn't want to scare him off. Which meant she wasn't truly being herself.

"Want some ice cream?" Nolan asked.

Ice cream? She was having an existential crisis. No, she didn't want ice cream.

"Do you think they have buttered pecan?" Daisey asked.

"I hope so," he said. "Dellie?"

"You don't like chocolate or vanilla?"

"Nope. I like the same as Mommy," Daisey said.

Of course she did, because Nolan kept her alive for his daughter.

"Ice cream?" he asked again.

"Yes. Strawberry with sprinkles."

"I want sprinkles too!" Daisey yelled, and Nolan took her off his shoulders and set her on the ground, taking her hand in his as they walked toward the ice cream stand.

Then he reached out and took her hand too. Her heart thudded so hard that she was pretty sure they could hear it all the way back in Chicago. His big hand holding hers suddenly assuaged all the fear that she'd allowed to wash over her. This was Nolan. He didn't mind her "excessive" personality or her impulsiveness. In fact, she was pretty sure that was what he liked about her.

So maybe she was being cautious for herself and not

because of her fear of his reaction. She leaned over and kissed his cheek.

"What was that for?"

"Just for being you," she said.

He seemed as if he was going to ask her more questions, but they'd gotten close enough to read the ice cream flavors and Daisey wanted to know them all. She laughed as he read them aloud. Sadly there was no buttered pecan.

"I guess I'll have strawberry like Delaney."

"What? No rocky road like Daddy?" he asked.

Daisey shook her head.

"I see that you have a new favorite," he said to her.

She just smiled and hugged his legs. "I'll always love you best, Daddy."

Delaney felt tears stinging her eyes, and she had to turn away. This was why she was afraid. Could she really be a part of a family that was this close and this honest? She wanted to be. It was the one dream that she'd kept secret her entire life. She'd pretended it didn't matter and had deliberately made each failed attempt at finding a family of her own seem as if it was no big deal.

But it had been.

And now she had to step out of all of that messy past and move forward with Nolan. It was time to come clean about Malcolm and the photos because she wanted no secrets between them when she told him she loved him. Maybe then she'd have a real chance at something more permanent with him.

He handed her ice cream to her, leaning over to kiss

her. Her blood felt heavier in her veins, her breasts fuller, and there was a warmth all over. She wanted him.

Daisey walked between the two of them, chattering about the things they'd seen. And Nolan looked over at her, catching her eye, and she felt a surge of emotion pass between them.

"Sorry you're not the favorite," he said with a wink.

"She's known you her entire life and me only a few months...give me some time to work my magic," she quipped.

"Is that what you do?" he asked.

"Isn't it?"

"I don't know about Daisey, but you have certainly cast a spell on me."

She didn't want him to think it was a spell, but she knew he was being flirty and took it as that.

"Tonight after I get back from my meeting and Daisey goes to bed...you're mine."

The committee meeting had been scheduled for late afternoon, and he left Daisey and Delaney on the steps of the Capitol with a wave. He was confident that whatever their findings, going forward the bidding process would be aboveboard. But there was no way they could ignore the fact that Malcolm had information before the rest of the field.

Also, the way the last few days had gone, he couldn't help feeling like his life was coming back on track. Workwise, the recent bid losses had been just one of the regular ups and downs of the business cycle, but he was glad to be on top again. Glad to finally be moving toward that success that he craved after all the hard work he and his team had put in.

The other part…well, the thing with Delaney was harder to process. She fit into his life with Daisey so completely that he didn't want to accept it. But the truth was she felt like the piece that had been missing for years. Not that he and Daisey couldn't have continued on as they had been—he knew that they could have— but the fact that she felt so right in their little family made him realize that she might be the one that he thought they'd never find.

And that made the hair on the back of his neck stand up. He hadn't allowed himself to think of a time when he'd find love again. And Delaney was so unexpected that he felt even more unsure.

"Cooper. You're a chip off the old block. Your old man always liked to be part of the next big thing. Been seeing you all over the place recently. You are really going hard after the publicity for the mission to Mars," Malcolm Quell said, coming over and offering his hand.

Nolan shook it and smiled at the other man who he hadn't seen since his father had died—their lunch meeting had never happened because of Malcolm's schedule. "My dad was a true pioneer and hero. And it was time to let the public know what they could expect from my company."

"Classic Delaney. Am I right?" he asked. "She's a master at crafting a message in a quippy little sentence."

"That one was me," he said. Not sure he liked how familiar Malcolm was with Delaney. Which was stupid because he knew they'd been a couple. And he wasn't a man to be jealous.

Except he was. Right now, he was fighting the instinct to punch Malcolm for no other reason than he'd mentioned Delaney. Which also wasn't his normal MO. So he turned toward the chamber where the committee meeting would be held.

"I think we better get in there. Any idea what the findings are?" Nolan asked.

"Not a clue. But then they have been playing things a lot closer to the vest on this latest bid," Malcolm said.

"Do they normally not?" he asked.

The other man shrugged. "Might just have been because I'd been dating Delaney and her cousin is on the committee, but let's just say some information had come my way early."

Delaney's cousin had been leaking information to Malcolm? He doubted the senior senator from New York, Darien Bisset, would have done that. He was known for his integrity. "Did Darien Bisset feed you information?"

"Never. He's too straitlaced for that. But certain tidbits used to come my way via other people. I assumed that Delaney had arranged it. You know how generous she is," he said.

Nolan did know how generous she was. But this went beyond doing something nice for someone and strayed into the illegal. Had she used her family connections to help Malcolm? He almost wanted to believe it because then he could believe she was too good to be true. But everything he'd come to know of her in the months they'd been working together made him hesitate.

They were shown into the chamber, and Malcolm of course knew everyone and went over to shake Darien's hand. But the other man kept the handshake short and then turned to the rest of the people filling the chamber. There were other space contractors like himself and Malcolm. Not everyone who was doing work for the Mars missions were billionaires, but most of them were. It was a big-money game and even getting these government contracts wasn't for any old start-up.

"Thank you all for joining us today," Darien Bisset said as they all took their seats. "We had an issue raised about the leaking of bid parameters and the award process, which is of course a concern. The Mars missions are a joint international project, and everyone who is bidding needs to feel confident that it is a level playing field."

Everyone around him sort of nodded, but Nolan sat still, waiting for the findings. Given what Malcolm had said about Delaney, he wasn't too sure what the outcome would be. Would Quell Aerospace be held accountable?

"Through the process of our investigation, we found that one of the bidders and previous winners was being fed information, including details of other companies' sealed bids, therefore eroding the process. We will be cancelling the awarding of those contracts and inviting companies to rebid and taking the perpetrator out of the running. My assistant will be handing out the new information at the end."

Nolan raised his hand.

"Yes, Mr. Cooper?"

"Which company was doing this?" he asked, not wanting to wait any longer for the answers he'd come here for.

"Quell Aerospace. Malcolm, we don't know to what extent this information was shared with you, but the members of your bidding team all were found to have direct contact with the office that oversees the contracts."

"What? That's an outrage! I have always followed the rules."

Sure he had. Hadn't he just mentioned in the hallway that he'd used Delaney's connections?

"I'm sorry that not everyone on your team seemed to do the same. Of course, you can file an objection, but we won't be considering you for the current bids."

The committee broke up an hour later. Malcolm stopped him as he was leaving.

"I can't believe this bullshit," Malcolm said, seething. "Seems like the kind of thing Delaney would instigate."

It didn't sound anything like the woman he knew who seemed to genuinely go out of her way for most people. "I doubt she'd have any interest in the bidding process."

"She's got her hands in plenty of things. You can never really read her. Watch your back, Cooper, or you could find yourself in the same situation as me."

He watched Quell walk away and had to admit he still had questions about Delaney. She had the information that Malcolm did, and she'd looked over his shoulder at his emails... Had she been playing him all along?

"What should we make daddy for dinner?" Daisey asked her after they'd gotten back to the house, and had both showered and changed into the matching T-shirts they'd purchased from a street vendor. They'd even gotten one for Nolan.

Delaney had gotten hers oversize and belted it at the waist to make a dress out of it. Daisey had loved the idea so much that she'd copied her. Then she'd braided the little girl's hair so that they could have the same hair per Daisey's request. Delaney couldn't help hugging the little girl. Deep down in her heart, she knew she'd fallen in love with Nolan's daughter too.

"What does he like to eat?"

Daisey shrugged. "Flo—that's my nanny—says he's too healthy for her."

If only Flo had seen him eating either the hamburger at his club or the Italian beef the other day, she'd revise that opinion. Healthy. Hmm...she wasn't sure what to make. She wasn't much of a cook, but she knew that Paisley was. "Do you mind if we ask one of my friends for some advice?"

"I'd love to meet your friends," Daisey said, hopping onto the couch next to her. Delaney video called Paisley with Daisey leaning over her shoulder. Paisley was still in the office when she answered.

"Hey, Dellie! How's DC?"

"Good. This is Daisey. And we are making dinner for Nolan but need some suggestions," she said.

"Hiya, Daisey. What does he like?" she asked.

"Something sort of healthy and easy for us to make. You've got two novice cooks here," Delaney said.

"And colorful. Daddy likes colors on the plate," Daisey said.

"Veggies?" Paisley asked.

She nodded.

Paisley suggested they make a pasta primavera for dinner and lemon ice for dessert and texted the recipes. Delaney thanked her friend and Daisey waved goodbye to her before they ended the call.

"Let's go and get some groceries."

They made quick work of the shopping trip and then got back to start preparing the meal. Daisey was a ball of energy the whole time, talking about everything and changing subjects quickly, which kept Delaney on her toes.

Nolan texted them he was heading back to the house, which sent a thrill of excitement through Delaney. Daisey kept running to the front door to look through the side window to see if he was home and then back to the kitchen to tell her.

Stanley loved the game and followed her back and forth, which made Daisey laugh.

"Seems like I missed some of the fun," Nolan said as he came in, kissing his daughter on the head and petting Stanley.

And Delaney felt like this was too good to be true. But she wanted this moment to last forever. She knew it wouldn't. It never did but maybe…maybe this time, right?

"Heya." She greeted him with a warm smile. "We're making dinner. Daisey set the table on the patio, and I need just ten minutes to finish this up," she said.

"You two look great. Where'd you get those shirts?"

"We got you one too," Delaney said. "Daisey, want to show him?"

"Yes!" she said.

They left and she finished cooking, and it wasn't until they were sitting at the table eating that she realized he hadn't met her gaze since he came home. But then he looked up and winked at her. "This is my new favorite dish."

"Is it? We weren't sure what you liked," Delaney said.

"Except colors," Daisey said.

"That's right. Got to eat the rainbow," he murmured to his daughter. "Veggies are Daisey's favorite."

"Is that true?" she asked Daisey. Surely he was exaggerating.

"Yes. I love them all, but bubble gums are my favorites," she said, gesturing to the lima beans on Delaney's plate.

Daisey had insisted they buy them at the store. "Bubble gums?"

Nolan shrugged. "That's what she calls them."

She realized that by making vegetables the main focus of the meals, he'd raised his daughter to love them. Personally, she only liked carrots and the occasionally grilled artichoke. But she wasn't about to be the only one at the table not eating them so she dug in, surprised at how tasty they all were.

After dinner Nolan set his camera up on the table at Daisey's insistence and used the timer to take a photo of all of them, including Stanley, who wore a red, white and blue bandanna. Then they had dessert and Daisey crashed, falling asleep on Delaney's lap as Nolan was reading to them.

"She's had such a long day," he said as he lifted her up and carried her into the house.

Delaney followed him, wondering how his meeting had gone. She knew she had to catch up on the business and help him plan for whatever announcement came out. But for this moment she wanted to just enjoy this family time.

She stood in the doorway as he tucked his daughter in and turned back to her. He caught her hand and pulled her into the hallway.

She put her hand on the side of his jaw and knew without a shadow of a doubt that she loved him. Not like she'd thought she'd loved Malcolm or any other man before. This was…overwhelming and safe and made her feel warm and toasty inside. Like she was enough… that this was real.

"I love you," she said. The words just came out without any thought, but she didn't regret it.

He stared at her, and she wondered if it was too soon. She knew she should regret it, but she couldn't. It was how she felt, and keeping it inside wasn't something she could do any longer.

She went up on her tiptoes and kissed him, and the passion that was always between them took over. He carried her down the hall to his bedroom, closing the door behind them.

Nolan growled deep in his throat as soon as they were alone. There was something primal about him tonight. She leaned forward to brush kisses against the side of his throat. Loving Nolan had freed something inside her, and when he carried her into the bedroom, she couldn't wait for him to make love to her.

She pushed his T-shirt up over his head, her hands aching to touch his chest. She kissed that Saint Christopher's medallion, and Nolan groaned aloud, his hands going for the belt she'd wrapped around her waist. He took it off, dropping it to the floor and a minute later, her T-shirt followed.

She stood there in front of him in just a pair of panties and some wedge sandals. His hands went to his waistband, unzipping his jeans and pushing them down his legs with his underwear. She traced each of the muscles that ribbed his abdomen and then slowly made her way lower toward his erection.

"All that healthy eating has paid off."

He grinned. "You like?"

"I just told you, I love."

He brought his mouth down on hers again, his tongue pushing deep into her mouth as he lifted her with his arm wrapped around her hips and carried her to the bed. He dropped her on it and then came down on top of her. He pushed her legs apart and tested her readiness before thrusting deep inside her and filling her completely. She closed her eyes and arched her back as she felt him start moving.

Stars were dancing in front of her eyes, and she felt her body tightening as she got closer to her orgasm. He kept driving into her again and again. Delaney reached for his head, pushing her fingers into his hair, pulling his mouth to hers. She sucked on his tongue as she felt her orgasm start. He kept driving into her, harder and faster, and then he tore his mouth from hers and grunted out her name as he thrust into her a few more times. She held him close to her, whispering that she loved him.

And as she slowly came back to herself, she realized with a pang that he hadn't said the words back.

She leaned up. "I guess you don't feel the same?"

"I'm not sure what I feel."

Fifteen

Nolan wasn't prepared to have this conversation, at least not now. He needed more time to process everything that had happened today. He'd let down his guard and the barrier that he always kept around his heart where Delaney was concerned. He wanted to let himself just fall in love with her and hope that would be enough.

But Malcolm's words hadn't fallen on deaf ears. He'd known that Delaney was complicated from the first moment that they met. After all, it was her connection to both Malcolm and her knowledge of the mission bid parameters that had set off red flags...leading to him raising his concerns to the bidding office.

And now...well, he was holding her in his arms and the most vulnerable part of himself, the part he pretended didn't exist, was afraid that if he tried to keep her, he'd lose her.

Wouldn't it be easier to just let her go now?

"Nolan?"

"Sorry, I'm not sure what to say," he admitted gruffly.

"If you don't know, then I think we both do," she said, getting off the bed and pulling her DC T-shirt back on. She picked up her underwear and the belt she'd had on and stood there with her arms crossed over her middle, watching him.

He'd never seen that look on her face before. There was pain and anger, and he hated to admit it but it hurt him to know he was causing her pain.

"It's more complex than that," he said. He was normally a blunt, no-nonsense man, but with her he was hesitating, stumbling over the truth. That wasn't fair to either of them. "Malcolm raised some things about you today that I can't ignore."

"What things?" she asked.

"That he thought he got inside information because of his relationship with you," Nolan said flatly.

"How is that even supposed to work?" she demanded. "I don't know anyone in the office that solicits and awards the bids."

"Your cousin does."

"Have you even met Dare? He'd never—and I'm not saying that lightly—share information illegally. He always takes the high moral ground." She shook her head. "Did Malcolm mention his former VP of Sales is now working in the procurement office?"

"No, he didn't," Nolan said, sitting up and putting

on his boxer shorts. There was clearly more to this than Malcolm had let on. "Honestly, I didn't really feel comfortable talking to him about you."

"Thanks for that. But it still obviously stayed in the back of your mind. You don't want to trust me, do you?" she said.

He wasn't sure. It would be easier—safer—if he could find a way to break things off before fate intervened. He knew he was afraid to love. Afraid to let himself believe that he could have a family with Delaney. He'd never been able to hold on to one. Not as a child after his father had died and not as a man after his wife had passed away. He had Daisey and he would always keep her safe, but Delaney was another story.

How could he protect her? How could he trust her to stay? Why wasn't this easier?

"I want to trust you," he said at last.

She shook her head and came closer to him. Tossing her belt and panties on the bed. "Then do. It's that simple."

If only. "I wish."

"Is this more about me not being someone you expected?" she asked with hope in her eyes and in the tone of her voice.

She wanted this to work.

Did he?

Yes.

And no.

His silence went on too long, but he had no idea what to say. This was the first time in his adult life that he'd been standing at a crossroads and didn't know what to do. And he knew it was his fear that held him back.

If he only felt lust for her, then yes, he would trust her, but he felt so much more than that.

"Nolan."

Their eyes met, and he could tell that the good grace she'd been giving him was waning.

"Yes?"

"If I had proof that the leak came from Malcolm, would you trust me then? Or is this something more? You didn't acknowledge my earlier question."

The way she was offering proof made him feel like an idiot. "No. I don't need you to show me proof that the man who has been getting inside information is lying. The hard part of all this isn't so much that I don't trust you. I think I do."

"Then what *is* the hard part?" she asked. "I love you. I hope you know that it's not easy for me to tell you that. I know we are very different people, but I want to take a chance on us."

She wasn't going to pretend she hadn't revealed what was in her heart, and he admired her for that. But he'd always had a hard time letting anyone in, and Delaney was no different.

"The hard part is knowing that love isn't always enough. That sometimes trusting myself is the hardest thing to do."

She stepped back from him, shaking her head. "I never thought you were a coward."

"Coward?"

"Afraid of love. What do you think will happen if you admit that you and I have something special?"

He hated that she'd called him on it. It fueled his anger, and even though he knew his words would hurt her, he said, "That you'll find someone else and move on to the next man."

Delaney was furious. At herself. At Malcolm. But mostly at Nolan. She knew her past relationships weren't necessarily a good track record. Still, she was sure that he was coming at this fight motivated by something else. But what?

And did she really want to keep throwing her heart at a man who clearly didn't want it.

No.

"I guess there is nothing more to say." She picked up her stuff and turned away. Sure, she could sling rude words back at him and yell and stomp and fight. But in the end that would never change anything, and it wouldn't make her heart hurt any less.

Choking back a sob, she went down the hall to the bedroom she'd been using and showered off the smell of Nolan. Then ordered an Uber while she packed her things. She heard a sound in the hall and looked up to find Nolan in the doorway.

"Are you leaving?"

"Yes. I'll send the jet back for you and Daisey to take you home. Just tell her I had a work thing come up."

"No. I don't want that. Can't we take some time here?"

She shrugged. "What time do you need? I know my

feelings won't change, and a lifetime of knowing my dad has proven that love…"

"Delaney."

"Nolan."

There was a sadness in her voice that she couldn't hide. A part of her wanted him to know he was responsible for putting it there. His phone starting pinging with alerts, as did Delaney's.

"Saved by the bell," she said, handing him his phone while grabbing hers.

She glanced down at her screen and saw her phone was blowing up with notifications about Malcolm. She skimmed them, and in the corner of her eye, she noticed that Nolan was doing the same thing.

"It says here that Malcolm is releasing a statement in the next hour—what happened today?"

"A lot," he told her. "We haven't had a chance to discuss it. But Malcolm was found to have underhanded dealings, his contracts were canceled and he can't bid on the current contract."

"Wow, that's just…wow. I can write a statement for you to release. I'll send it over to Hal. You should be—"

"Delaney, *stop*. I don't want to talk about that now," he bit out.

"There is nothing else to talk about," she said. "You know that and now I do too. I need to get Stanley's food…" She trailed off as she realized she was leaving this man and this little family that she'd hoped would be her own. Tears were burning in her eyes, and she blinked quickly to keep them from falling. She had been here before, but in the past it had never hurt this bad.

She needed to put on her dish soap heiress face and get out of this house before she crumpled.

"You don't have to go," he said hoarsely.

Delaney remembered her father's inherent disapproval of her and straightened her spine. So no matter what, she wouldn't let Nolan see how much he'd hurt her any more than she'd let her dad. She whistled for Stanley, who was sleeping on his blankets in the corner. When he trotted over to her, she put his leash on him then scooped up his bedding and tossed it in her suitcase. She just wanted to get out of here and away from Nolan.

"I'll get the dog's food," he said at last.

As soon as he left, she knelt and buried her face in Stanley's neck and wiped the few tears she couldn't hold back against him. Then she kissed her sweet dog and made sure she hadn't forgotten anything before walking out of the room with her bag and dog.

Nolan waited at the end of the hall with Stanley's food and his bowls.

"I'll send some notes over to Hal—"

"Don't. I can handle this. You've done enough," he said.

"So now that we're over, you don't need me to work with you?"

"I was trying to make it easier for both of us. I think we both need a few days," he said.

"Why? Will a few days really make a difference?"

He tightened his jaw; his hands were clenched in fists by his sides. "I'm sorry. I don't always know how to handle my emotions."

"You're a grown man, Nolan. Figure it out," she said. "Tell Daisey I said goodbye."

Her app let her know the Uber was there, but she would have left even if it hadn't been. She stepped out of the house and walked to the car with Stanley at her side. The driver got out to take her bag, and she was tempted to look back but couldn't. She wanted to blow Nolan a kiss or something else to show him that he hadn't gotten to her. Hadn't broken a part of her that she'd always protected.

But he had, and she couldn't pretend he hadn't. Delaney got into the car, and Stanley followed her and jumped up on the seat and on her lap. On the way to the airport, she texted her pilot and he'd said he needed a few hours to meet her, which was fine.

She was starting to breathe now that she was away from Nolan. But her heart was still sad, her soul shattered from trusting him, from believing he was different from every other man in her life.

That he'd somehow been able to recognize that she wasn't really broken, just misshapen, when it came to love. But instead, he'd proved to her that she was. That she was unlovable even when she let her guard down and was her true self.

That hurt more than she wanted to admit. Unlike Malcolm, he'd needed nothing from her—not her money or family influence—and maybe that was why he hadn't wanted her in the end.

She didn't know.

Didn't like the downward spiral that her mind was going in. But she was also powerless to stop it. In the old days, she would have drunk until her mind got numb, but not anymore. Now she dug in her huge shoulder bag, finding the notebook her therapist had recommend she carry, and she wrote all the negative thoughts down. Got them out of her head. Later, when she was back in Chicago, she'd rip them out of the journal and burn them and then write down the positive things.

And slowly she'd start to heal.

"Where is Delaney again?" Daisey asked him at breakfast the next morning.

"I already told you she had to go back to Chicago because of work. You know I'm not her only client," he said. "She said to tell you goodbye."

"I wish I had got to say goodbye to her," Daisey whined.

"I know she would have wanted that too." He couldn't help but blame himself for this. He hadn't thought of his daughter when he'd let Delaney walk out the door and go back to Chicago without them. He could try to justify it and tell himself that she'd get over it, and he knew eventually she would, but he still deeply regretted how things had gone down.

His phone started blowing up with messages, and he looked down to see that Malcolm Quell had been arrested. Apparently, the insider information wasn't all he'd been using to win bids. He'd attempted to bribe Darien Bisset's assistant, and she'd turned him in to the police.

Wow.

"Pip, I'm really sorry about this," he said. He meant

this trip and the stuff with Delaney but also that he was going to have to work and not just play with her today.

"That's okay. When will you be talking to Delaney?"

He should be texting her right now. She was his right hand when it came to the press, but he'd hurt her and said some things he shouldn't have and told her they should take some time. "I don't know."

"Why not?"

Daisey got down from her chair and came over to his side. He pulled her into a fierce hug, then pulled away and turned to face his daughter.

"I hurt her feelings last night," he admitted thickly.

"Daddy. Did you say sorry?"

"I did, Pip, but it was too little too late," he said.

"You have to make this right. I like her."

If only it was that easy. "I do too, but this isn't going to be easy."

"Daddy—"

"I'm not giving up on her, but I have to take care of this work stuff first," he said, knowing of the two, work would be easier. Hal was calling in, and he hit the button to send it to voice mail.

He had to make sure Daisey was okay first. Then he got a text from Delaney with some bullet points that he should use when he talked to the press. Still being professional as she always had been with him.

He took the bullet points that Delaney had sent and texted them to Hal before calling his PR manager. He spent over an hour on the phone discussing it and preparing a press release while Daisey colored on the floor next to his desk. They'd decided a press conference would be too showy, but he had a comment ready for the media if they sought him out.

He was ready to figure out his next move with Delaney, but Darien Bisset called and asked if he could come by his office.

"I can, but my daughter is with me and I'd have to bring her," he said.

"That's not a problem. The Capitol press pool will probably have questions. I'll ask my assistant to meet you out front, and she can bring your daughter to my office. I am inviting the other primary bidders, as well. My office wants to issue a statement with all of you so that the public knows the Mars projects are still going forward with integrity."

"What time do you need me over there?"

"Does forty-five minutes work? I was hoping to get to you before the news of Quell's arrest was made public," he said. "The press always gets word the moment something happens."

"I'll be there. Can you text me your assistant's name?"

Senator Bisset did as soon as they hung up.

"We're going back to the Capitol, Pip."

"Who's going to watch me?"

"Senator Bisset's assistant. Is that okay?"

She sighed. "I guess so."

"How about if I take you to the zoo after and we get ice cream?"

"Strawberry with sprinkles?" Daisey asked, naming Delaney's favorite and now his daughter's.

"Yes," he said, knowing he had to find a way to fix this. For the both of them.

"Thanks."

The rest of the day was a blur of press conferences and discussions with the other Mars mission contractors. Everyone had questions, and the answers the government gave were reassuring. He was exhausted when he got done, and Daisey was tired too and just wanted to go home.

Delaney had texted him that the jet was back and ready for their use. They flew back and arrived home at midnight. He tucked Daisey into bed and then finally had a chance to think about Delaney.

Nolan wanted to text her, but really, after what he'd said to her, they had to talk in person.

He felt like an idiot for repeating Quell's accusations to her. But he had. And now he had to figure out how to fix that.

Delaney was so generous and her heart so big, that he hoped she'd forgive him, but he wasn't sure. He'd taken her declaration of love and threw it back in her face. Told her that he couldn't trust her feelings, and that had to have stung.

He *knew* it had.

He'd seen the tears she'd tried to hide, and he'd done nothing. Used his own fears to feign indifference and tell himself she was trying to fool him. When in the end there was no one to blame for his foolishness but himself.

He wished there were a way he could go back and act better. Be better.

He heard Merri's laughter in his head. And he felt reassured. He'd screwed things up with her when they were dating, he remembered. But he'd won her back by being honest and humble and letting her know that he needed her in his life.

It was time he let his guard down for good and did the same thing with Delaney.

He loved her.

Nolan realized he'd made a huge mistake in not trusting her, but also in selling himself short. In letting his fears dominate his actions instead of his heart.

He had no idea how to fix it, and it was Saturday after they'd gotten back home when he finally realized he needed some help. Daisey had been moping around since they'd gotten back to Chicago. Both of them missed Delaney terribly.

"Pip, I'm going to need your help to show Delaney how much I want her back in our lives—"

"*We* want her back," Daisey said.

He smiled and kissed his daughter on the forehead. "We do."

Nolan knew that he was going to have to show Delaney how much he loved her in a big way. But seeing how much Daisey loved her and wanted her back in their lives made him realize that she was the woman he'd been waiting for.

Sixteen

Delaney went into the office the following day, surprising both Olive and Paisley when they arrived. She'd gotten to the office early since she hadn't been sleeping anyway since returning from DC. Even Stanley seemed to miss Nolan and Daisey.

"What are you doing here?" Olive asked from the doorway.

"Working," she said with a smile. She'd even put on her most businesslike outfit to reinforce her #bossgirl vibe. A white crop top under a hot pink blazer and matching trousers with high-heeled mules that were green with pearl accents. Then she'd pulled her hair into a low bun and had put on her fashion glasses with the large frames.

"Why? We thought you were in DC," Olive said as

she came farther into Delaney's office and set down the stapler she'd been carrying.

"What was that for?"

"In case you were an intruder," Olive said.

Paisley set down her hole punch and they both turned to stare at her. Waiting.

So how to spin this? She had no clue. She was doing her best to fake something she wasn't sure she was ever going to be again.

"Things were said and I came home."

"What things?" Paisley asked.

"Yeah and stop trying to be cool," Olive said. "You only dress in what you think is business attire when you are really upset. We're not your dad, you can be yourself with us."

Sighing, she took off the oversize frames. Then, putting her hands on the desk in front of her, began frowning when she noticed she had a chip in her manicure.

"Dellie, what is it?"

"He didn't love me," she sobbed, and even though she thought she'd shed all the tears last night, more started to fall. Her friends were at her side in a heartbeat, hugging her. Both talking at the same time.

"I'm sure that's not true. Maybe he's afraid to admit how much he cares," Olive said.

"He doesn't deserve you if that's the case!" Paisley declared.

Her friends, these sisters of her heart, made her both feel better and cry a bit harder. She wished that either of them were right. "I just think something inside of me is unlovable."

"Stop that," Olive chided. "There isn't anything broken in you. You are the only way that you can be. There's nothing wrong with that. If I can find love after being the meanest bitch on the planet, you definitely can."

"But I wanted it to be with Nolan and Daisey. I think I love her as much as I love him," she admitted to her friends.

"Let's sit on the couch," Paisley said. "Tell us exactly what happened."

They moved over to the couch and sat down with Delaney in the middle. "We had the best few days, doing the touristy thing, and really I just felt like I could be me. I didn't once worry if I was too much or not enough."

"Good, that's how it should be," Olive said.

"So how'd it all go south?" Paisley asked gently.

Of her two friends, Paisley was the more practical. "Um, he went to a committee meeting and Malcolm was there and got in his head. Malcolm suggested that I was the reason why he'd been given insider information."

"That rat!" Olive said.

"Bastard," Paisley added.

"I know, right?" she said. "But that doesn't matter. Malcolm can't change who he is. It was Nolan's reaction that mattered."

"And he believed Malcolm?" Paisley asked.

Olive's phone was lighting up with notifications, which happened all the time since they were in the brand and spin business. They had to stay on top of all the gossip and scandals.

"He didn't not believe him. Does that make sense?" Delaney asked.

"Get your phone, Dellie. Malcolm's been arrested!" Olive said.

Delaney went to her desk and saw the notifications coming in about Malcolm. She was glad he'd been arrested. He deserved it for being so sneaky and underhanded. "I should send some talking points to Nolan."

"Are you still working for him?" Olive asked. "I would have told him to kiss my butt and walked away."

"Of course she's still working for him," Paisley said. "She won't give him the satisfaction of knowing he hurt her."

"You're right. He did say to take a few days so we could adjust to not being together, but this needs my attention. I'll chat with you girls later."

"Drinks on the patio in my office tonight," Paisley said.

Her friends left, and she started working on the topics she thought the press might ask Nolan. Once she had a draft, she sent it to him with nothing other than that. No personal message because she wasn't ready to put on a good face with him.

The rest of the day went by quickly. She reflected on how seeing Malcolm get what he deserved didn't feel as good as she'd thought it would. It just made her sad to think of his employees who might be affected by his actions. And a little bit disappointed in herself that her judgment had been so faulty that she'd thought she'd been in love with Malcolm Quell.

When the way her heart and soul felt today proved

that entirely false. What she'd felt and frankly *still* felt for Nolan was making her body ache. She didn't know how she was going to get over him. And the fact that she'd gotten over Malcolm so quickly showed her how shallow that love had been.

She realized that for the first time she was really in love. This was like nothing she'd experienced before, and she had no idea how to deal with it. As the day wound down and she went to meet her friends for drinks, she knew that they had no solution, either. This kind of heartbreak was going to take a long time to get over, but for tonight hanging with her friends and having their support made her feel a little less alone.

Nolan had made up his mind to go and see Delaney, so early the next morning he texted Perri that he was taking the day off. He didn't want anything to distract from Delaney and what he needed to do to win her back.

Daisey came into his bathroom and sat on the counter while he shaved. "Make sure you tell her you're sorry. Daddy, are you sure I can't come with you?"

"I will and I am very sure. You have school today," he pointed out.

"I know, but I don't want you to mess up."

"I promise you I won't," he said. Nolan had made up his mind to do whatever it took to show Delaney how much he cared for her. He just wished he'd been able to see it before she'd walked out the door. But it had taken losing her for him to realize how much he needed her to stay.

Daisey just nodded at him, and when he was done

shaving and had wiped the leftover shaving cream from his face, he turned to her. "How'd I do?"

She put her little hands on his face and nodded. "Nice and smooth."

"Thanks, Pip," he said, hugging her close.

He got Daisey ready to go to school, and as soon as she was out the door so was he. He had thought about a big romantic gesture or maybe something public, but over their courtship he'd realized that her false self was the one she portrayed to the media. The real woman was more of a homebody and liked to stay in with her dog and her friends.

So he wanted to show her how well he'd gotten to know her. He had texted Olive and Paisley and asked them if they would get Delaney to stay home today. And though both were reluctant when he told them he needed to make things right, they'd agreed.

He stopped at Delaney's favorite coffee shop, the one she always ordered from when they had an early appointment, and got her favorite latte. And then knew there was no more stalling. He had to go and see her.

The walk to her front door felt like the longest he'd ever taken. And he realized he wouldn't blame her at all if she couldn't forgive him. Just the uncertainty of what she might do was almost enough to make him turn around. But he knew that the bigger the risk, the bigger the reward.

He rang the bell and heard the sound of Stanley barking and wished he'd brought something for her dog too. Then the door opened and she stood there in one of those long, flowy dresses she favored. Her blond hair hung around her shoulders and her face was free of makeup. Stanley went up on his back legs, and Nolan bent to pet the dog who, once he'd had some attention, turned and trotted back into the house.

He straightened and looked at Delaney, who arched both of her eyebrows at him. "What are you doing here?"

"It's been a few days and we need to talk," he said. Then realized how all business he sounded. But that was his default. When he wasn't sure, he went into CEO mode.

"What if I don't want to?"

He sighed. He hadn't expected this to be easy and didn't blame her if she wasn't ready. "Then I will wait until you are."

She shook her head. "I'm not nearly ready to do this, Nolan."

"Fair enough. But I think you know that I'm not one to back down when I want someone." He handed her the coffee he'd brought for her.

"Fine." She huffed out a breath. "Come in and let's do this."

Delaney turned, leading the way into her house. She went into her living room, which was as eclectic as she was, and he sat down on the overstuffed chair she'd gestured to.

"What do you have to say?" she asked. He could tell she was nervous because she kept turning her coffee cup in her hands as if she wasn't able to sit still.

"That I'm an idiot."

"You're not. It would be easy if you were, but you're

a very smart man so that means at some point you believed I was using you," she pointed out.

"No, that's not it. I mean, at first I wasn't sure what was going on with the information you had, but what really held me back from trusting you was my fear of letting you into my life," he said.

"So why did you? I thought DC was supposed to help us both figure that part out." She slid him a hurt look. "Seems to me you figured it out one way and I did another."

"No, we both did the same, but I wasn't ready to admit it."

"And now you are?" she asked doubtfully.

"Yes," he said, getting up and going over to her. He took the coffee cup out of her hands and set it aside before he sat on the ottoman in front of her. "I have been falling for you from the moment you turned to me at the wedding. But I wasn't expecting it and I had no idea how to handle my emotions. Or yours."

"You're falling for me?"

He smiled and nodded. "Actually, *have* fallen. I was afraid to let you in because I don't know that I'm strong enough to lose you. I have always been part of a family that is out of balance, and what Daisey and I have worked until I saw you with us in DC. But that just made me more afraid."

"Fear is a funny thing," she admitted. "So Malcolm's words of warning about me?"

"As I said, it was a nice excuse to end things. It gave me a safe out, but as soon as we talked, I knew you wouldn't ever do anything underhanded like that. That's not your way. You'd walk right in and tell me whatever you'd found out. That's what you did after all."

"It is," she said. "So, what did you figure out?"

"That I love you. I should have told you that before you left DC," he rasped. "I know that I treated your heart badly, and if you need time, you have it. But know that I'm yours and I'm not going anywhere."

"For now? What if someone else accuses me of something?" she asked.

"I'll stand up for you and have your back," he promised. "I did it with Malcolm but not with you."

"You did? When did that happen?"

"After the committee meeting…but that doesn't matter. He doesn't matter. *You* do. I should have told you how I felt."

"And you love me?"

"Yes… I love you, Delaney."

Her lower lip trembled. "A-are you sure?"

"You know me. I don't say things I don't mean."

"Oh, Nolan, I love you too!"

She threw herself into his arms and they fell back on the floor. He held her close in his arms. "From the moment I saw you, I knew my life was never going to be the same, but I had no idea the joy that waited for me."

She put her hands on his face and kissed him. "Me too."

Nolan held Delaney's soft weight on top of him, enjoying the feel of her in his arms. He hadn't been sure of how long it would take, but in his soul he'd known he would win her back because he never stopped until he got what he wanted, but he hadn't known how long it would take.

He wanted her, and as much as he thought they should make love and it should be special, he also kind of just needed to be inside her and claim her for his own. Reassure himself that she loved him and wanted him in her life.

He pushed her dress up, caressing her back and spine. Scraping his nails down the length of it. He followed the line of her back down the indentation above her backside, drawing small circles there until she raised her torso and looked down at him.

He took a deep breath, inhaling her sweet scent and relishing it. "I want you."

"I want you too," she whispered, then she leaned forward, resting her forehead against his. "I was afraid I'd never kiss you again."

"I'm sorry. I wish I hadn't been an ass."

"Me too," she said.

He kissed her then, rolling them to their sides so he could deepen the kiss and still hold her close to him. Then he undid the tiny buttons at the front of her dress and pushed it down off her shoulders. She shoved it all the way off, and he realized that she only wore a pair of lace panties under her dress.

He fondled her breasts, running his finger over her nipple. It was velvety compared to the satin smoothness of her skin.

Delaney let out a husky moan and he brought his mouth down hard on hers, swallowing her sounds. She pushed him onto his back and stripped off her underwear while he freed his erection. Then she climbed on top of him and he sat up to wrap his arms around her as she wound her legs around his hips and took him deep inside her.

She tipped her head to the side, her hair brushing against his back as she moved on him. He tried to hold back and let her set the pace but couldn't. Instead, he put his hands on her hips and drove himself up inside her, taking her hard and fast. It took every bit of his self-restraint, but he held back his own orgasm until he heard her cry out his name. Her body tightened around his as he finally emptied himself inside her.

"Ah, Delaney," he said. "You have enchanted me."

"Is that a good thing?" she asked, and he heard the hesitation in her voice.

"It's a *great* thing. You remind me there is more to life than just living," he said.

"You were doing a pretty good job of that without me, scheduling your fairy hunts and Ginger Rogers movies with Daisey."

"That was for my daughter. I almost felt like I didn't deserve anything for me," he admitted.

"You deserve it all, Nolan. We both do, and together we're going to have it all."

No woman had ever seen him the way she did. That she had forgiven him and taken him back was more than he expected, and he knew he'd never take her for granted ever again. They spent the day together talking about their future and went together to pick up Daisey from school. His daughter ran to Delaney and hugged her legs.

"I missed you."

"I missed you too," Delaney responded.

"I told Daddy to get you back."

"I'm glad he did."

Nolan lifted Daisey into his arms, then gathered Delaney close, knowing that he had everything he needed right here in his loving embrace.

"I am the luckiest man alive," he said.

"Yes, you are," Delaney agreed with a smile in her eyes.

* * * * *

Look for the next novel in
The Image Project trilogy

Billionaire Fake Out

Available next month!

#2923 ONE NIGHT RANCHER

The Carsons of Lone Rock • by Maisey Yates

To buy the property, bar owner Cara Thompson must spend one night at a ghostly hotel and asks her best friend, Jace Carson, to join her. But when forbidden kisses melt into passion, *both* are haunted by their explosive encounter...

#2924 A COWBOY KIND OF THING

Texas Cattleman's Club: The Wedding • by Reese Ryan

Tripp Nobel is convinced Royal, Texas, is perfect for his famous cousin's wedding. But convincing Dionna Reed, the bride's Hollywood best friend...? The wealthy rancher's kisses soon melt her icy shell, but will they be enough to tempt her to take on this cowboy?

#2925 RODEO REBEL

Kingsland Ranch • by Joanne Rock

With a successful bull rider in her bachelor auction, Lauryn Hamilton's horse rescue is sure to benefit. But rodeo star Gavin Kingsley has his devilish, bad boy gaze on *her*. The good girl. The one who's never ruled by reckless passion—until now...

#2926 THE INHERITANCE TEST

by Anne Marsh

Movie star Declan Masterson needs to rehabilitate his playboy image fast to save his inheritance! Partnering with Jane Charlotte—the quintessential "plain jane"—for a charity yacht race is a genius first step. If only there wasn't a captivating woman underneath Jane's straightlaced exterior...

#2927 BILLIONAIRE FAKE OUT

The Image Project • by Katherine Garbera

Paisley Campbell just learned her lover is a famous Hollywood A-lister... and she's expecting his baby! Sean O'Neill knows he's been living on borrowed time by keeping his identity secret. Can he convince her that everything they shared was not just a celebrity stunt?

#2928 A GAME OF SECRETS

The Eddington Heirs • by Zuri Day

CEO Jake Eddington was charged with protecting his friend's beautiful sister from players and users. And he knows *he* should resist their chemistry too...but socialite Sasha McDowell is too captivating to ignore—even if their tryst ignites a scandal...

HDCNM1222

Get 4 FREE REWARDS!

We'll send you 2 FREE Books plus 2 FREE Mystery Gifts.

FREE Value Over **$20**

Both the **Harlequin® Desire** and **Harlequin Presents®** series feature compelling novels filled with passion, sensuality and intriguing scandals.

YES! Please send me 2 FREE novels from the Harlequin Desire or Harlequin Presents series and my 2 FREE gifts (gifts are worth about $10 retail). After receiving them, if I don't wish to receive any more books, I can return the shipping statement marked "cancel." If I don't cancel, I will receive 6 brand-new Harlequin Presents Larger-Print books every month and be billed just $6.30 each in the U.S. or $6.49 each in Canada, a savings of at least 10% off the cover price, or 6 Harlequin Desire books every month and be billed just $5.05 each in the U.S. or $5.74 each in Canada, a savings of at least 12% off the cover price. It's quite a bargain! Shipping and handling is just 50¢ per book in the U.S. and $1.25 per book in Canada.* I understand that accepting the 2 free books and gifts places me under no obligation to buy anything. I can always return a shipment and cancel at any time by calling the number below. The free books and gifts are mine to keep no matter what I decide.

Choose one: ☐ **Harlequin Desire**
(225/326 HDN GRJ7)

☐ **Harlequin Presents Larger-Print**
(176/376 HDN GRJ7)

Name (please print)

Address   Apt. #

City   State/Province   Zip/Postal Code

Email: Please check this box ☐ if you would like to receive newsletters and promotional emails from Harlequin Enterprises ULC and its affiliates. You can unsubscribe anytime.

Mail to the **Harlequin Reader Service:**
IN U.S.A.: P.O. Box 1341, Buffalo, NY 14240-8531
IN CANADA: P.O. Box 603, Fort Erie, Ontario L2A 5X3

Want to try 2 free books from another series! Call 1-800-873-8635 or visit www.ReaderService.com.

---

*Terms and prices subject to change without notice. Prices do not include sales taxes, which will be charged (if applicable) based on your state or country of residence. Canadian residents will be charged applicable taxes. Offer not valid in Quebec. This offer is limited to one order per household. Books received may not be as shown. Not valid for current subscribers to the Harlequin Presents or Harlequin Desire series. All orders subject to approval. Credit or debit balances in a customer's account(s) may be offset by any other outstanding balance owed by or to the customer. Please allow 4 to 6 weeks for delivery. Offer available while quantities last.

Your Privacy—Your information is being collected by Harlequin Enterprises ULC, operating as Harlequin Reader Service. For a complete summary of the information we collect, how we use this information and to whom it is disclosed, please visit our privacy notice located at corporate.harlequin.com/privacy-notice. From time to time we may also exchange your personal information with reputable third parties. If you wish to opt out of this sharing of your personal information, please visit readerservice.com/consumerschoice or call 1-800-873-8635. **Notice to California Residents**—Under California law, you have specific rights to control and access your data. For more information on these rights and how to exercise them, visit corporate.harlequin.com/california-privacy.

HDHP22R3

HARLEQUIN PLUS

Announcing a **BRAND-NEW** multimedia subscription service for romance fans like you!

Read, Watch and Play.

Experience the easiest way to get the romance content you crave.

Start your **FREE 7 DAY TRIAL** at www.harlequinplus.com/freetrial.